To Kate

Hope you enjoy
reading

Lisa Parkinson

Life, Love and Holiday

LISA PARKINSON

authorHOUSE®

AuthorHouse™ UK
1663 Liberty Drive
Bloomington, IN 47403 USA
www.authorhouse.co.uk
Phone: UK TFN: 0800 0148641 (Toll Free inside the UK)
        UK Local: 02036 956322 (+44 20 3695 6322 from outside the UK)

Published by AuthorHouse 06/25/2021

ISBN: 978-1-6655-8852-2 (sc)
ISBN: 978-1-6655-9053-2 (e)

Chapter 1

Their Adventure Begins

Lizzie was the girl who everyone knew of, but no one really spoke to at school. Although that was the way she liked it. She didn't have many people she would call true friends, and she was certainly unlucky in love. She was the type that might have a couple of dates, but she had never experienced that spark or warmth she thought she would want to feel within. In her eyes, no one so far was worthy of her time or of the title "boyfriend". Her best friend, Meg, had experienced what she thought was love. She had lost her virginity at the age of sixteen to her boyfriend of six months. The next day he ended things with her. As Meg entered the school lunch hall, he called her over to the table where he sat with his group of friends. He told her, "It's over now that I've got what I wanted." The guys all gave him a high-five and laughed at her. She was completely embarrassed and ran out of the hall crying. After that both Meg and Lizzie were very cautious about whom to trust.

Now, two years later and finishing college, they were still the same. However, there was one major difference; they were happy with their lives. They had both learnt from

Meg's experience. They knew they didn't need a guy to make them feel content. They hadn't stopped dating, but they were waiting for the right person to even contemplate a third date, let alone anything else. Lizzie knew that the person she chose to call boyfriend would make her feel special and make her body tingle with warmth just by standing next to her. She knew that he would understand and accept everything about her. Meg and Lizzie were not about to settle for anything less.

Lizzie and Meg were the type of people who would blend into the background. People only saw them if they really wanted them to. They thought themselves rather plain and certainly not the prettiest in the class. Lizzie had very dark, wavy hair, dark eyes, and was small framed. Meg, too, was small framed; she had light brown, straight hair and blue eyes. Unlike the popular girls, they didn't wear makeup very often, especially for school. They had started listening to rock and alternative music, whereas most of the people in their year enjoyed dance or trance. That style music gave Meg and Lizzie headaches, so socialising with the rest of their year group didn't really happen.

They had met in the first year of primary school and very quickly became best friends. They did most things together. They used to play tennis on a Tuesday, have a meal out together on a Wednesday, and over the weekend, they would go for a run or a bike ride. Despite going to the same school, they spoke most nights. Their college years were a little different as they did end up having separate lessons. Lizzie loved biology and health, whereas Meg was determined to go into wildlife rehabilitation. Their only shared lesson at college was biology.

They were both looking forward to and dreading their university years as things were about to become very different. Meg was going to a university in Scotland, and Lizzie was going to be at the opposite end of the UK, near Southampton. They were dreading being so far away from each other but were eagerly anticipating not being with the people from school. No one they knew was going to the same universities, and they were looking forward to just being themselves. First though, they were looking forward to their summer holiday.

Six months ago they booked themselves a holiday after their exams and had been looking forward to it ever since. It had given them something good to focus on and aim for, rather than everything just being about studying. They had booked a two-week all-inclusive holiday to Spain. Just the two of them, sun, sea, and sand. They opted for all-inclusive as they wanted no worries about money and what they were doing. It was time to relax, drink, and get a tan. The complex had everything, and the beach was only a ten-minute walk away. There were swimming pools, tennis courts, and most important, it was for adults only.

Lizzie and Meg were checked in, their cases handed in, and they were waiting at the departures security desperate to go through, eager to start their adventure. First they had to endure the long parental speeches of, "Be safe," and, "Look after each other," and, "Don't forget to let us know when you arrive." At security there were lots of young adults in the same boat, all trying their best to show their parents that they were listening when actually all they wanted was to go through and get away from their parents. Eventually,

Meg managed to say, "Right. I'm starving. We're off to find somewhere for dinner."

Meg and Lizzie knew their parents were only worried about them. They understood and were trying their best to listen and respond appropriately. But in the backs of their minds, they were just thinking how much they wanted to start their holiday. And they were really hungry.

As they went through security, they were free, alone at last. Their holiday had started. They collected their bags from security, waved to their parents, and disappeared round the corner. Then they burst out laughing. They looked at each other with the mischievous, excited, "Yes, holiday," expression. They were being silly, laughing, joking, and not paying any attention to their surroundings. Lizzie, not paying any attention to anything at all, managed to bump into someone.

As she bumped into him, he was knocked off balance and stumbled slightly. During the collision, Lizzie ended up looking straight down at his feet. He had big, black boots with lots of buckles and zips. She couldn't help but smile; they were very similar to hers. Her eyes continued upwards, noting his long, black, baggy trousers that got tighter around his pelvis with plenty of rips, zips, and pockets. Her spine was already tingling with anticipation. Her gaze stopped at his stomach. She bit her lower lip as she could see the tight T-shirt clinging to his well-defined abs. His pectoral muscles and biceps made her involuntarily take in a sharp breath. Her gaze rose to his shoulders, which were at her eye level. At this point, she was so nervous she couldn't look up any farther. She dropped her head in embarrassment, apologised in a rushed voice, and walked off quickly.

During all this, Meg was far too busy crying with laughter at Lizzie to pay any attention to anyone around her. Lizzie was a very clumsy person, and Meg was always laughing at her when she did things like this. As they walked off, Meg was still laughing, and it made Lizzie laugh too. They finally found somewhere to have dinner and enjoyed the time waiting for their flight. While they sat having food and a couple of drinks, Lizzie was mentally kicking herself for not looking up at him, for not making eye contact. She and Meg talked about how nervous Lizzie had become about seeing his face, especially considering how she felt just seeing the rest of him and how tall he was. He had seemed perfect for her, his clothes and his boots. Now she was gutted because she would never see him again. Meg suggested walking around while they waited for their flight to see if they could find them, but they had no luck.

The guy Lizzie had bumped into had stood waiting for the usual stupid comment he always heard from girls. He was shocked when she basically ran off. He looked at his mate, who had been too focused on Meg to really notice Lizzie, but he had also seemed shocked when the girls went off without really saying anything to them.

"What just happened?" Lizzie's 'victim,' asked his mate with a confused, puzzled expression.

"I've no idea. No stupid comment about your biceps. You losing your touch?" he joked. They picked up their bags, hoping to pursue, but as they looked up, the girls had disappeared in the crowd. They walked off in the same direction Lizzie and Meg had, trying to find them, but they didn't succeed.

Finally the flight was ready to board. Lizzie and Meg

were so excited that they hadn't even realised how late it was or how tired they had become. They walked down the aisle and found their seats. They busily sorted out things to get ready for the flight and pushed their bags under the seats in front. They had pulled out some sweets and most important, their books. This made them smile because they both just pulled out the same book. "Great minds think alike," Lizzie said.

They both enjoyed reading, and they had a lot of similarities when it came to their interests. They discussed what other books they had brought. Two out of five books they had both packed were the same.

"We should have talked about this before packing. We could have shared!" Meg said, smiling with amusement. Lizzie giggled. They settled down, making sure they were as comfy as possible for the flight.

For the first half of the flight, they read their books, until the guy who was sat in front of Meg stood up and walked past them going towards the back of the plane. Lizzie saw how tall he was and stared at his face with a wide-eyed expression.

"Oh, my God! So hot!" she blurted out.

Luckily, Meg and Lizzie didn't have the same taste in men and had never crossed paths over a man before. But they did understand each other's type. Meg just smiled and then suddenly erupted in hysterics.

"What?" Lizzie asked, a stern, confused look taking over her face. "What is so funny?"

Meg was now uncontrollably laughing. Unable to catch her breath she just pointed to the seat directly in front of Lizzie. Looking round the seat, Lizzie saw a guy looking through the gap at Meg. He had a big smile on his face, as well as a wide-eyed shocked expression. He wasn't shocked by what Lizzie had said but more that she had said it so loudly. Lizzie buried her face in her hands. At this point, the guy came back and gave his friend a strange, quizzical look.

His mate pointed directly at Lizzie.

"Hi, I'm Harley," he said confidently to Lizzie and Meg as he knelt on his seat facing towards them. His mate did the same.

Lizzie looked up and smiled. In her head she was introducing herself, but instead her mouth just dropped open, and no words—none at all—came out. The corner of Harley's mouth raised into a little smirk. Inside, Lizzie felt like her body did a backflip and she took a sharp breath in.

"Hi, I'm Meg, and this is Lizzie," Meg stepped in, giving Lizzie a nudge as she said her name, hoping to save her from any further embarrassment.

"H-H-Hi," Lizzie finally managed to stutter quietly.

This made Harley chuckle. Then he introduced his friend, Luke.

"Hi," said Luke. "Hey Hars, isn't this the girl who bumped into you in departures?"

"Ha, oh yeah. You know, she completely took my breath away," he said flirtatiously. "Cruel really, making me lose my balance like that, and she couldn't even look me in the eye."

"Oh gosh, I am *so* sorry. I really am *so* clumsy, and then when I realised how tall you were I, umm, well." Lizzie was so nervous that all her words rushed out, seeming to blur into each other.

"That's okay. I forgive you now," he said with a cheeky but sexy smile that emerged at one corner again. Harley, in

Lizzie's eyes, was gorgeous; she couldn't stop staring. Lizzie was thinking of asking where they were stopping, but she didn't want the disappointment of knowing they were not in the same complex.

It was announced over the speakers the plane would be landing soon, and everyone needed to take their seats. Harley gave Lizzie a heart-melting smile, a smile that made her shudder inside. Then he turned to sit down. Luke was more subtle, giving Meg a little, shy smile. Meg returned his smile, her cheeks colouring slightly. Lizzie looked over and saw that Meg was nervous. She was biting down on her thumbnail with her incisor, a coy expression on her face.

As the plane stopped and the passengers were told they could deplane. Almost everyone jumped up. Meg and Lizzie decided to follow whatever the guys did. Harley and Luke were busy packing up their things, so they hadn't stood up yet. Eventually, with very few people left on the plane, Meg and Lizzie stood up and grabbed their bags. When they looked up, they noticed the guys had just started walking down the aisle.

Harley and Luke were going slowly. They were busy talking and seemed to take turns checking to see where Lizzie and Meg were. Harley was taking the mick out of Luke, who had just admitted he fancied Meg. Harley knew that before Luke said anything. Luke did get his own back, though, as it was very obvious from the way Harley had flirted with Lizzie that he really liked her. Luke and Harley knew each other really well. They had one thing in common with Lizzie and Meg: They didn't date. Harley hadn't actually been on a single date with anyone, and he certainly never deliberately flirted with anyone.

The four continued to walk together. They were talking about silly things all the way to the bag collection carrousel. Spotting her bag, Lizzie approached the carrousel, but Harley offered. She told him which bag and let him collect it for her. As he picked it up off the carrousel and placed it on the floor next to Lizzie, he commented on how heavy it seemed. "How long are you away for?"

"Only two weeks. Not long enough."

"Are you sure it's only two weeks?" he joked showing his wonderful sexy smirk. "That case is heavier than mine and Luke's combined."

"You're boys, though. Bet you've hardly brought anything."

Harley laughed.

Meg and Luke had been talking and as her case came round, Luke collected it for her. "Would you two like some help to your coach?" he offered.

"That's OK. We can manage, but thank you," Meg responded.

The guys seemed saddened. So was Lizzie, but she also understood why Meg had said no.

"Well, enjoy your holiday," Luke said.

"Yes, thank you. And you too," Lizzie and Meg said together, making Harley and Luke laugh.

They went their separate ways to find the transport to their complexes. Lizzie and Meg found some seats on their coach. "I can't believe we didn't ask where they were staying," Lizzie said, rather gutted that they would never see them again.

"Would you really want to know? It's not likely they would be at the same place as us." Meg had liked Luke, but she was more discrete. They joked about how good it would be if the guys got on their coach now and how gorgeous they thought they were.

Just then a soft, deep voice interrupted with, "Hi, again." As they looked up, they saw it was Luke, and Harley was walking up the coach aisle. Harley gave his sweet, sexy smile again, melting Lizzie into a heap. She had been having an internal battle with herself since the flight. A warmth had been trying to build, but as she assumed she wouldn't see him again, she had been trying to ignore it. But seeing Harley on their coach, this feeling suddenly spread throughout her. Meg was in a similar state and couldn't help but stare at Luke. An excited smile spread across her face, and her eyes had lit up. Both girls were so excited and happy that Harley and Luke were on their coach, and that meant they were all stopping at the same complex. Lizzie smiled back at Harley, who was just taking his seat next to Luke. Then she looked at Meg and shared an expression of *Oh, my God*.

The four talked all the way to the complex. Lizzie and Meg didn't stop smiling the whole journey of about an hour. Their hearts didn't stopped thumping in their chests. Both were intoxicated by the gorgeous guys who sat across from them and were actually paying them attention.

Harley was a good foot taller than the girls. He had dark eyes, and his dark hair was in an all over ruffled, dishevelled, spiky style. They talked about how Lizzie and Meg knew each other. Luke and Harley told them they were brothers. Harley's mum had met Luke's dad about twelve years ago and were married a few years later. Harley and Luke had been thrown together, but they ended up best mates, despite their differences, although they added they had a lot a similar likes now too. Luke was only a little taller than Meg. He had piercing blue eyes and blonde hair that was long on top, pulled into a rough forward, side sweep with shorter sides. Like Lizzie and Meg, they had just finished their A-levels and were looking forward to a holiday to celebrate it was all over.

Luke did most of the talking. Harley seemed to be a man of very few words. Actually, Harley was also having his own internal battle. He didn't date for a good reason. Any girl who had shown interest in him was usually only after one thing, a one-night stand or popularity. Harley had created a barrier against this which he was now struggling to maintain as, for the first time, he fancied someone and wanted to get to know her.

The hotel reception area was very grand. It was decorated in different shades and blends of white, cream and brown. It looked like a granite or marble, and it had shiny flecks in it which created a wonderful sparkle. From the reception a stream could be seen running through the centre of the complex. It was a manmade stream with blue, white and silver tiles along the sides and base. Each side had a ledge. The flowing water shimmered in the moonlight. The bar was quiet, although it was late. It had a quiet, cosy corner with large, comfortable-looking sofas and chairs. There was a dance floor on the other side, with a small stage next to it. The bar itself was small, and the moonlight reflecting off the swimming pool created a magical shimmer.

Once checked in, Luke offered to help Lizzie and Meg to their room, but they wanted to wander slowly, take in their surroundings, so they turned down the offer. They were also trying to keep themselves from getting too carried away.

They did, however, casually agree to meet up tomorrow for drinks round the pool. This holiday wasn't about making plans, but it was obvious they all wanted to meet up again. Harley and Luke just wanted a drink, so they went straight off to their room, getting drinks from the bar on their way. Lizzie and Meg took in their surroundings, marvelling at what they could see around them. As they walked through the bar, they, too, stopped to get drinks to take to their room.

Lizzie and Meg had their drinks while they chatted and unpacked. They wanted to get the boring bit out of the way, so they could relax and enjoy their holiday from the moment they woke up tomorrow. The room was comfortable and cool. There were two single beds in the bedroom and two two-seater sofas in the lounge area. The door to the bathroom was between the lounge and bedroom. It was a lovely, big bathroom, with a large all-in-one bath and shower. They spent the whole time unpacking just talking about the guys, until they suddenly stopped and looked at each other.

"This isn't like us, Lizzie. We never get hung up on a guy like this!"

"I know. This is definitely not like us. Maybe tomorrow we need to take a breather, have that drink with them, but steer clear for the rest of the day," Lizzie responded in a very serious tone. They looked at each other and burst out laughing, collapsing onto their beds. "I don't think that's going to be possible," Lizzie said through her laughter.

Meg sat up on the edge of her bed. Her expression had turned serious. "Lizzie", she said, taking a deep breath, "I've not felt like this ever, not even with Dave." Dave was the idiot she lost her virginity to when she was sixteen. She thought he was everything back then—until the day he ended things. From that point onwards, she realised what an idiot he was and what an idiot she had been for letting herself be taken in and used like that.

"Meg, I think we need to be careful."

"Yes, I agree."

"But it would be nice to have a holiday romance, if that's what happens," said Lizzie.

"Being honest, I really want Luke. But I, … I get the impression that if I made a move, he would back off."

"Well, no plans, remember? It's not like us to let a guy determine our happiness. But Meg, follow your gut. If he wants you—and he does—he will make it happen. You've just got to let him know that's what you want too. That might give him the confidence to make that move."

"Thank you. What about Harley? I can't seem to figure him out."

"I don't know. We will probably talk and be friends, but he wouldn't go for someone like me. He's gorgeous and could have his pick." She paused. "But Meg, I think I'm going to struggle. Whenever he gets close to me or smiles at me, I get all warm and tingly. And I just can't think properly."

"You really like him, don't you?"

"I don't think really, really covers it."

Meanwhile, Luke and Harley had reached their room, which was laid out the same as the girls' room. "Harley, what is going on with you?" Luke demanded as he dropped the case on his bed.

"What do you mean?" Harley was confused by Luke's statement.

"You know exactly what I mean. You and Lizzie. I've never known you so quiet and timid."

"Yeah, right. I was not." Harley was getting defensive.

"Hars, you hardly said anything, and normally you're the centre of things."

Harley sighed and collapsed backwards onto the bed. Lying there, hands over his face, he sighed again, realising that what Luke said was the truth. "You're right! I have no idea what is going on, but that Lizzie is just ..." He sighed again. "She's gorgeous. She has literally taken my breath away. I can't think. I feel absolutely pathetic. No girl has ever made me feel like this."

Harley sighed again and took a good deep breath to regain himself. "Anyway, you can talk. What about you and Meg?"

"I know." Luke smiled. "She is lovely, and it sounds like we have loads in common. I can't wait to see her again tomorrow."

Harley and Luke grabbed what they needed out of their suitcase and went to sleep, without unpacking.

Chapter 2

The First Day of the Holiday

After breakfast the next morning, Lizzie and Meg went exploring the complex. They found the route to the beach, the tennis courts, and the pools. By lunch it felt like they had been there for days. After lunch they went for a cooling and relaxing swim.

Later that afternoon, they went to the bar and bumped into Harley and Luke, who were playing pool. Luke was definitely dressed for his holiday in colourful shorts and no top. His muscles were immense. It was Meg's turn to be speechless. She just was stood there, her eyes were wide, and her jaw had dropped. Lizzie gently nudged her back to reality. Meg smiled and shook her head slightly. Harley, not dressed for a sunny holiday, was in black shorts and a tight, dark grey T-shirt which made his well-defined biceps stand out. Lizzie was biting her lower lip again, a slight smile on her face, while she imaged those muscles being wrapped all around her, sending her all gooey feeling inside.

Luke saw them and waved, and the girls waved back. Lizzie went to get drinks for them both while Meg sat at the table closest to the pool table. While waiting for the drinks, Harley approached the bar. They had finished their game, and Luke had gone to sit with Meg while Harley got the drinks. Harley seemed less confident than he had been on the plane. "Hi Lizzie," he said, but his voice was softer, more like a whisper. The bar was only small, a column was to her right, and a man sat nearby to her left. Harley stood between Lizzie and the man. The gap was so small he had to stand at an angle. He was stood facing Lizzie, with his side and lower arm resting on the bar. They were so close, she could smell his aftershave; he smelt so good. She took a deep breath, trying to not become overwhelmed by his scent, but it didn't work. Nothing had worked to calm the intensity she felt every time he was close by.

The bartender placed Lizzie's drinks on the bar and took Harley's order. They had been talking, mainly about who won at pool, so Lizzie waited for Harley's drinks to arrive too. Harley continued the conversation by asking what music Lizzie liked, and they ended up talking about their favourite music groups. They had much to talk about with music, as they both enjoyed rock, although Harley was also into heavy metal.

Lizzie stretched out her arm to move the drinks closer, ready to take them over to the table. At the same time, Harley happened to move his hand slightly, causing their hands to brush together. He saw her facial expression alter, her body tense, and it made him smile. He smiled because he instinctively knew that he had just cause a pulse of electricity to flow from her hand through her entire body. He knew this because that was what he also experienced. Their eyes met and fixated on each other. For a moment Harley started to lean in. However, the drinks arrived, and they were snapped back to reality before he had been able to get too close. Neither of them knew why they felt so intensely drawn to each other. Neither of them had ever been in this type of situation before.

They picked up the drinks and took them over to Meg and Luke. On the way, neither of them said anything. They were both too busy trying to regain control of their impulses. Harley was cursing himself. He had never, not even once, felt this type of desire, and all he could think was, *Why now? Why Lizzie? And why can't I be my normal, confident self around her?*

Lizzie was feeling similar emotions. She wondered, *Why now? Why him? What is so different about him compared with any other guy I've dated?*

While Lizzie and Harley were at the bar, Meg and Luke had been talking a lot. He sat very close to Meg, so close his knee was almost touching Meg's knee, and his body was fully facing her. He leaned on his elbow that rested on the table, so he could sit forwards, leaning in towards her. She had placed herself comfortably in the chair with her body leaning towards him, almost mirroring his posture. Intermittently, Luke would run his fingers lightly over Meg's arm or knee, and she would smile.

Lizzie could see the hesitation in Meg's eyes and hoped that Luke could not. Meg wasn't hesitating because of Luke; she was hesitant because of her past and because she didn't want to be the one to make the first move.

Harley and Lizzie walked over and placed the drinks on the table. It was a small table, so the four all sat quite close. Lizzie sat next to Meg, and they gave each other a smile. Harley sat on the chair between Luke and Lizzie. As he did, he positioned the chair so that it was closer to Lizzie. He kept looking over at her. Lizzie wondered, *Why does he look so puzzled?*

Harley was actually trying his best to understand what was going through his mind and why he was drawn towards Lizzie so much. But in the end, he gave up thinking about what all this meant and just decided to test her. He wasn't testing to see if she liked him; he could already tell that she did. But Harley's track record with girls was problematic. Most of them only wanted him for his looks, not caring about him. Harley wanted to see if she actually wanted to get to know him.

He leaned in towards her, placed his hand on her knee, and whispered in her ear, "Would you like to play a game of pool with me?"

She looked him in the eyes. He was so close, and their breathing had changed due to how the intense chemistry was taking hold of them. Harley seemed to hesitate and then bit his bottom lip, at which point Lizzie answered yes. Harley breathed a small sigh of relief and smiled.

There was only one pool cue, and it was obvious from the first time Harley handed Lizzie the cue that he was using it to get close to her. But he maintained his self-control and distance, at least to begin with. He actually just wanted to grab her and kiss her, but that wasn't him. And it wouldn't answer his question. He had never done this before; to be honest, he had never wanted to either. His barrier had served him well, but now, with Lizzie, it was failing. He started talking about music first, following up from their conversation at the bar.

Lizzie had a couple shots but had to apologise as she

didn't play pool. She had been trying to maintain a bit of distance, trying not to become overwhelmed again. But eventually he began to make subtle, deliberate touches. When she handed him the cue, he made his hand meet hers. He occasionally placed his hand on the small of her back or ran his fingers down her arm. He could see the effect his touches were causing. He could see her muscles contracting or her sudden, sharp breath she took as the pulse of electricity flowed through her, just like it flowed through him.

He went over to take a gulp of his drink and stood there for a moment. He just stood looking intently at Lizzie. His question had been answered. From their conversation he realised this wasn't about a one-night stand or just trying to make herself feel good. She actually seemed to want to get to know him, and that made him nervous about what to do next. It was his first time doing something like this, and she had punched through his confident exterior.

Luke went over to him, and they stood whispering to each other. "Hars, what is going on?" Harley just looked at him. "You need to just go for it. Make your move."

"How though? No, wait! Such a stupid question. I know how. I'm just—"

"Scared", Luke interrupted. "Welcome to my world."

Harley took a deep breath, releasing it in a slow, controlled manner. "Right. Back to me!" A determined look took over his face.

Luke just smiled. He knew exactly what Harley meant by that. Harley was normally confident around everyone, and this should be no different. He was going to go back to that pool table confidently and make his move.

He boldly strode back over. Harley took the cue from Lizzie and took his next shot. Lizzie hadn't been playing very well. She hadn't played much pool before, and when she leant over to take her next shot, he took over. He placed one hand on her elbow and one hand on her hand. She gasped.

"Lower your hand down the cue," he said. Gulping hard, she followed his instructions, but that feeling was building within her again.

He lowered himself over her. His head was in line with hers. His body was positioned over her back, and his hands were placed over hers. She had lost control now, her breathing erratic, her spine tingling, and she felt frozen.

"Position your gaze straight down the cue, and line up the white and the ball you are aiming for." He went round to the other side of the table.

She took a deep breath to steady herself. And as she looked at the white, she was also looking straight at him. He had crouched down and could see she was trying to do as he had said. "No, you need to lower your eye level. You'll find it easier." He smiled and went back round to her. He placed his hands to direct her back and shoulders lower to the table, so she was almost lying against the cue.

His touches were sending her senses into overdrive. She was trying her best to control herself, but it was not easy. Her breathing was deep and shaky with anticipation. She wanted more. Lizzie was struggling to move. Everything felt against her due to one thing: the feelings she was experiencing for Harley. She took a deep breath and held it. This gave her enough control to be able to make her shot. He stayed standing next to her as she took her shot, and as she stood up, he was still right there. They were pretty much standing on top of each other, facing each other. He was about a foot taller than her, but to Lizzie, it felt like he was towering over her. She was completely overwhelmed again by his scent, his firmness, and his closeness. By this point her breathing was so shallow and quick that her mouth and lips had become dry. She licked her lips, biting her lower lip in the process.

With everything going on, she had paid no attention to her shot or where the balls were. He took the cue and leant over to take his shot. She suddenly realised that he had put her between him and the cue. She decided to try to divert his attention from taking his shot, so she ran her fingers through his hair and down the back of his neck. It caused a reaction, but not in the way she thought it would. His eyes closed due to her touch, and it was his turn to bite his lower lip. Her fingers traced down his back, and she saw how his back arched slightly as his muscles contracted under her touch. Once her hand reached his belt, she stopped. He took a deep breath, regained his composure, and potted the black. As he stood up, he placed his free hand on the small of her back. Suddenly she felt those biceps in action as he drew her into him, their hips forcefully crashing together. Her hand had not moved; she had not yet had a chance to respond. As she shyly looked up, she saw him towering over her again, looking directly into her eyes. He was breathing just as deeply and slowly as she was, and there was an intense hunger in his eyes. All she could do was wait. She couldn't reach his lips even if she stood on her tip toes. But he was hesitating. After what seemed like forever, Lizzie reached up and brushed his cheek with her hand, but it had the opposite effect to the one she intended. Without saying a word, he relaxed his grip on her waist and went to hand the cue back in at the bar. Lizzie was left stood there, confused and deflated. As Harley walked back over, drinks in hand, he went straight to the table, not acknowledging Lizzie at all. Lizzie still stood at the pool table, feeling like she just wanted to run away. But she looked over. She saw how happy Meg seemed with Luke and decided she had to at least try to be friendly to Harley.

While Harley and Lizzie had been playing pool, Luke and Meg had been talking. Luke seemed more sensitive than Harley. He had been subtly getting to know Meg, giving little touches and brushes of her hands or knees during their conversation.

Harley had brought back four drinks from the bar, and they all sat chatting. An hour later, Harley seemed to be getting restless and asked Lizzie to go for a walk with him. Lizzie felt hesitant, especially after what happened at the pool table. But she knew that it would give Luke and Meg some private time, so she agreed.

They wandered down to the beach and paddled their feet in the sea. It was lovely and cooling. It had been such a warm day, and now, as the sun was starting to set, the sea breeze was cooling the air. There was hardly anyone around, and Harley had seemed to change. He became a more sensitive person and placed his arm around her shoulders, asking her if she was OK. Then the next thing she knew, he had stopped walking and was embracing her. It was such a tight hold that she seemed to melt in his arms and went all weak at the knees. She was trembling with desire. Lizzie could see that the hunger had returned to his eyes. He leant down towards her until his lips are hovering directly over hers. His warm breath on her exposed skin set her body on fire. His expression told her that he was feeling the same. His grip of her tightened, and he brought his other hand up to caress her cheek. It was obvious from her expression and deep breathing what he was doing to her, but he was still hesitating.

Once again he released his grip on her. He went over to sit on a sun lounger. She sat down next to him with a puzzled look on her face. She wasn't sure if she felt angry, if she was being messed about, or whether there was something else going on. She decided to give him the benefit of the doubt. She knew that no matter what happened between her and Harley, they would be spending time together because of Luke and Meg. "What is it?" she asked, her more caring side showing.

"You have no idea what you do to me, do you?" His voice was definitely less confident now. He seemed nervous as his hands rubbed together and fidgeted.

"Why don't you tell me? Or better still, show me?" His breathing was heavy now, and he looked almost guilty. "You have a girlfriend, don't you?" Lizzie asked, sadness taking over her.

"No. No, absolutely not," he said adamantly. He took a deep breath, held it for a few seconds, closed his eyes, and exhaled in a slow, controlled manner before opening his eyes again. "I …" He took a second deep breath, held it, and looked up, fixing his gaze on hers. They suddenly realised how close they were. As he breathed out, she felt his warm breath on her face, and his eyes were fierce and intense. Their breathing seemed to have fallen in sync.

He swallowed, and her eyes flickered to the movement his lips made because of it. As her gaze returned to his eyes, his have been caught in her movement; she was biting her lower lip again. He leant forward slightly, and she instinctively mirrored him. Their lips were so close. He arched his neck slightly, tilting his chin up, and their lips came closer, almost touching.

Her mouth had become dry again, and as she licked her lips, his gaze dropped to the movement again. Harley moved forwards, crashing his lips into hers and causing an explosion of pleasure. She kissed him back with fierce intensity, their desire coursing through their veins. He teased his tongue along her lips, forcing them to part. He let it brush over her tongue, causing even more explosions of pleasure. She slid her tongue over his lips and felt his teeth against it, causing more tingles down her spine. His hands suddenly clasped around her firmly. And then he stopped, pulling away to allow his eyes to focus on hers, and he smiled. It was not the sexy smirk she had seen before. It was a happy smile that told her, *Wow*.

"I was enjoying that," said Lizzie.

"Plenty more of that later," he said as his smile grew.

She smiled back. "Later sounds good."

Lizzie and Harley continued to walk, holding hands, for a while before heading back towards the complex. Suddenly, Harley sat down on a sun lounger and dragged Lizzie down with him. He deliberately pulled her off balance as he laid down, pulling her so she fell on top of him. She looked a little shocked, but then he ran his fingers through her hair, while his other hand, which was round her waist, pulled her in tight. He raised up slightly and kissed her. It was a delicate and warm kiss. Lizzie ran her fingers through his dishevelled hair, and as she slowly pulled away, she gently bit his lower lip. That made him freeze. She was worried, but then his look changed. His expression became deeper, more intense than it had been so far. His grip on her waist tightened, and he pulled her head towards him, sending their lips crashing together again. Their feelings were erupting. Their kiss was full of the overwhelming passion they had so quickly developed. There was no way of hiding how they felt about each other now. There was absolutely no going back.

"I, umm" he hesitated. "I've never felt this way before. You're amazing," he whispered in her ear. "I honestly don't know what you do to me." He then trailed kisses down her neck and back up to her lips. Lizzie's muscles were contracting with the sensations he was causing throughout her entire body. When he reached her lips, they seemed to become locked together in a warm and heartfelt kiss.

He finally loosened his grip slightly, and she was able to pull away just enough to focus on his gorgeous face. His eyes were deep as he looked longingly and meaningfully into hers. All she wanted was to kiss him all over again. But then a voice announced that the beach hut was closing and the sun loungers being put away. They had to move. Lizzie was surprised at how sad she felt that they couldn't just stay there longer. It had not even been twenty-four hours since they first met, and now they felt they couldn't be separated.

"Let's walk back and find Luke and Meg," he suggested with a little peck on the lips. He took her hand, and interlacing their fingers, they walked back.

On the way past the pool, Harley looked at Lizzie with an incredibly cheeky but sexy smile and pushed her into the pool. As she started to fall, she grabbed hold of his hand, something he hadn't anticipated, so they both went plummeting into the pool with an immense splash. It was dinner time, and the pool was being shut up for the night, so there were very few people around. As Harley came back towards the surface, he ran kisses up her stomach, chest, and neck before he emerged out of the water, and their lips crashed together. He could stand up, and he was using this to his advantage. He pressed his body against hers. Her body was pinned against the pool wall, stopping her from moving. His body gently brushed against hers as the waves of the pool caused their bodies to bob in the water.

Eventually, Harley helped Lizzie out of the pool, and they looked down at themselves. Realising they couldn't go back to the bar dripping wet, he took her hand, and they wandered around talking for a while. Just him brushing his thumb against the back of her hand was driving her body wild. They hadn't been paying attention to where they were walking until they walked into the enclosed area, and what sun was left, disappeared.

He looked up with disbelief and realised where they were. He pulled her back into the minimal sunshine. He took her round the waist and lifted her up, her legs cradling round him. He sat her on the low wall. His arms stayed wrapped around her in a close, gentle embrace. Sitting on the wall made Lizzie just the right height. She brushed her lips against his. But as he went to push his lips into hers, she moved and kissed him on the cheek instead. He swallowed hard, obviously trying to suppress a moan. She kept going, trailing open-mouthed kisses down his neck and along his collarbone. She had never done that before, but she just went with her instincts. Her teeth, tongue and lips glided along his skin. He moaned, his muscles clenched, and his grip round her waist tightened. He was enjoying what she was doing. She glanced up to focus on his eyes, but they were closed. Everything she did was adding to his arousal. Until suddenly, he backed off slightly.

He brought his hand up to rest on her cheek, his thumb stroking her skin. Her eyes instinctively closed as desire flooded through her body. Her body pulsated with the desire to feel him more. Her fingers were tangling in his dishevelled, damp hair, and she pulled him closer. His lips hovered over hers, sending more shivers down their spines. The hunger, with fierce intensity, was back in his eyes, and his strong hold was pulling her against his muscular form. It was his turn to trail his soft, wet lips up her neck. And when he reached her ear, he gently grazed his teeth on her earlobe. A breathy moan escaped her which caused him to stop. It was quite sudden, and she looked at him puzzled.

"It's only day one. Maybe we should get back to the bar," he said breathlessly, but as confidently as he could. But Lizzie could tell that he was only saying it as it was the right thing and not what he wanted. "I'll grab us some dry tops from my room. You can borrow one of mine."

"You're right. OK," Lizzie unwillingly agreed. She had wanted to stay there for as long as they could, but she also knew it was the right thing to do. After all they had only just met, and this was only the first day of a fourteen-day holiday.

He gently lowered her to the floor and took her hand.

When they entered his room, she closed the door behind her and waited in the lounge area, while he went to grab some tops. As he came back in, he looked at her. The hunger suddenly back in his eyes, he marched over, leant down,

27

and slamming their lips together, he kissed her deep and rough. That was it. They were both lost in the sensations shooting through their bodies, the waves of pleasure pulsing throughtout.

Chapter 3

Their First Time

He whisked her up into his arms as if she were as light as a feather. She wrapped her legs around him as he basically slammed her firmly against the door. He relaxed his grip with one arm and ran his fingers over her sides and through her hair. Not once had they broken the seal of their lips. He took all her weight in his arms and sat on the sofa. Lizzie was straddling him now, and as he lowered her onto his lap, she could feel exactly how aroused he was. He cupped her cheek and pulled her in for an open-mouthed kiss. Sliding his tongue between her lips, their tongues danced together. Every gentle touch, every passionate flick of his tongue was communicating exactly what he was feeling inside. Lizzie, now trembling with the built-up desire, could feel his member suddenly pulsate under her, and she thrust her pelvis hard against him, sending his head backwards with a gratifying moan. She kissed his Adam's apple and ran her tongue up to his chin.

Suddenly, with one quick move, he flipped her over, so she was lying on the sofa. He stood up, stripping off the still-wet clothes to his boxers. Then he stopped and looked at her, his breathing deep. He checked to see if she is all right with how things were going. He searched her eyes for some reaction but couldn't find any until she raised her arms above her head, and in just two swoops, her shorts and T-shirt were off. She was left lying there in her bikini. His eyes slowly looked her up and down, as if he were absorbing every part of her. He placed one knee between her legs, grazing her upper thigh and making her gasp while he lowered himself to kiss her neck. He was becoming rougher and needier with his kisses. His body firmly grinding against her.

Suddenly nervous, Lizzie blurted, "I've not done this before."

Those sudden and rather loud words make him stop. He raised up, locking his elbows straight to give her space and so he could focus on her properly. "Would you like me to stop?" he asked in a very soft, very kind voice.

"No," she said trembling, her expression full of sorrow for stopping the moment. She took a breath. "I'm sorry. I didn't actually mean to say that, that loud."

"This is your first time?" His voice was still soft.

"Yes. First for a lot of things in this last hour," she replied with a nervous giggle.

"Just so you know, I've not done anything like this before. It's actually my first time too."

"What? But you're gorgeous. How is this your first time?" she asked full of amazement. She believed he was telling the truth, but she was still amazed.

"I don't tend to attract the right girls, so I've always distanced myself. But you, you are different from anyone I've ever met before."

Lizzie smiled and ran her fingers through his hair. He

lowered on to his elbows and slowly, passionately kissed her on the lips for a moment. He lifted her up and continued to kiss her. The next thing she knew, her bikini top fell to the floor, and Harley was lowering them on to his bed. He had her so securely that she didn't feel unsafe at all. His hands slid from round her and past her hips. He took her bikini bottoms in them as he traced his fingers all the way down to her toes. He removed his boxers and climbed into bed, draping the sheet over them. He snuggled right up to her and started kissing her intensely again. His arms enveloped her upper body, while his leg curled around her legs, pulling her in tight. Their connected bodies now moved in sync, rubbing against each other, their hips gliding together. Lizzie couldn't take the building of pleasure anymore. She had never felt anything so intense. Her arms, wrapped around his shoulders, tightened. The sensations caused her muscles to contract. Her back arched, pressing her firmer into him. And all the while he hadn't stopped kissing her, everywhere.

He rolled her over so he was on top of her, supporting his weight on his elbows. Her arms still wrapped around his neck, she tried to pull him down against her, but he resisted. His open-mouthed kisses left fiery trails as he moved down her body, disappearing under the sheet. Her hands firmly grasped the sheet due to the sudden explosion of pleasure that surged through her as his tongue licked her right where she needed to feel him. He continued tantalising her, getting just the right spot. Her muscles contracted, her body shivered, and the overwhelming desire coursed through her. He slowly trailed more kisses up her body. And reaching her lips, he gave her a teasing smile.

He reached an arm out, picked up some protection, and

placed the packet against her lips. "Your choice. Could I make love to you?" he asked gently. He gulped as he realised what he actually said wasn't what he had intended.

The way he said it just made her want to say yes, but she knew he was letting her say no if she wasn't ready. Lizzie wasn't about to back out now though. The desire that he had stirred, the need she felt to have him, she wanted to make love to him; she wanted this overwhelming pleasure to continue. She also knew she wanted her first time to be with Harley. She knew it was too soon in their meeting, but she also knew that so far, everything had felt right. She had been wanting this since they met on the plane.

She bit the packet with her teeth, and Harley tore it open, leaving the packet in her teeth while he placed it on. Then he took the packet from her and ran it gently down her body. Lizzie had experienced all the teasing she could handle. She seized his shoulders with her arms and wrapped her legs round him. She tried to pull him down onto her, but again he resisted. Her breathing was uncontrollable now. She didn't just want him, she needed him. "Please", she whispered through gasps, her eyes fixed on his. He was biting the corner of his lower lip and smiling his cheeky, sexy smile. She tightened her legs around him and pulled down with all her strength.

He didn't resist this time. Instead, he slowly, and in full control, lowered his body firmly against her. Their lips clashed together in an enthusiastic and passionate way. He held her, positioning himself in the perfect position. As his member brushed her now immensely sensitive spot, he stopped to focus on her. "Are you OK? Are you sure you want this?"

"Yes," she almost shouted, trembling with the anticipation of what was to follow, and as he slowly slid in deep, she let out a pleasurable moan.

"You OK?" he asked, but Lizzie had lost all use of her voice and just nodded her response. He began his rhythmic, slow, deep movements, their bodies bonding with fluent, smooth movements. Their rhythm increased in velocity and force. The headboard of the bed clashed against the wall. Harley was using his elbows to support most of his weight off Lizzie. But when she pushed his elbows outward, he couldn't hold himself up as easily, and his additional weight dropped on her. Her moans intensified with this, and she dug her nails into his back, which caused a pleasurable, painful moan to escape his lips. Their movements became even more forceful, neither of them seemingly able to be satisfied.

Suddenly, she moaned loudly as an intense and explosive climax took hold. He slammed his lips against hers to muffle the moans. A few movements later, he reached his own climax. Loud grunts escaped his lips, before he collapsed his head down on to the pillow next to Lizzie. His body still pulsating from his climax. Harley had a sudden, overwhelming pang in his chest that spread throughout his whole body. He had to hold his breath. He closed his eyes, and his face scrunched slightly, trying to stop himself from blurting out the feelings he was struggling with.

They remained in the same positions for a while. Their bodies had lost all control. Once he had recovered some feeling in his body, he moved to the side and pulled Lizzie into a tight embrace. "That was amazing. You're amazing," said Lizzie.

"I really like you. You are amazing," he whispered.

Chapter 4

After

During their after-sex cuddles, Harley tried to process everything going on within him. He knew he *had* to have her. He knew he needed her. And he also knew that this was just a holiday, and he was going to have to protect himself. But he didn't want to.

Lizzie was going through her own inner turmoil. She didn't believe in things like love at first sight, but it was the only thing that seemed to explain the sensations that were trying to burst out of her.

Several cuddles later, after they both seemed to find their inner controls, they decided that Meg and Luke might be wondering where they had got to. Their clothes were still soaked through. Lizzie put her bikini back on, and he threw her one of his T-shirts to wear. It almost drowned her, looking more like dress than a T-shirt on her. He had been hanging the clothes in the bathroom, and as he walked back out, he saw her in his T-shirt. "I like that on you," he said with a wide smile. Lizzie laughed.

Harley took Lizzie's hand, interlocking their fingers, and they walked back to the bar. Just before they reach the bar's entrance, he wrapped his arms around her waist, and stopped them. "I meant what I said. You're amazing, and I really do like you."

"I think you're amazing too." She paused as Harley looked down at her, leaning his head so their lips brush together. "And I ... I've never felt this way before." As she spoke, her lips glided over his. Then he closed the minute gap completely in a slow, pleasurable kiss, ending with him biting her lower lip. As he pulled away, they made eye contact, staring intently, both mesmerised. She licked her lower lip, drawing it under her upper lip, once again savouring his minty flavour.

Harley and Lizzie entered the bar and found Meg and Luke in a lip lock. Luke's arm was around Meg, and the other was brushing her cheek. Harley pulled Lizzie back slightly and took her over to the bar. "Luke hasn't found anyone he likes enough to make a move since, oh umm. Let's grab some drinks before we go over."

"Since what?" Lizzie asked curiously.

"I shouldn't have said anything."

"Harley, I need to protect my friend. Please."

Harley knew he had already said too much. With Lizzie he kept having to stop himself. He felt comfortable with her, and he just wanted to tell her everything. He knew that was going to lead to problems, especially in these very early days.

"Well, he had his heart broken about eighteen months ago. He fell hard for a girl slightly older than us. She used him for a month, and once she completed her bet, she moved on."

"What was the bet?" Lizzie questioned, with a sad expression.

"She and her mates were all playing a game. They each picked a guy in the bar, and the first one to have sex with them won. But it couldn't be a one-night stand. It doesn't sound like it should have been difficult. After Luke gave in, we discovered that the girls had each gotten to know their guys for about a week and then turned on the charm to make the guy have sex. One of the other girls had won the bet the first week. So she had just been stringing Luke along so that she could lose her virginity before she went to uni. Our parents had been away for the weekend, and he invited her over. She turned up naked with a coat wrapped around her. When he answered the door, she took her coat off, dropped it on the floor, pushed him onto one of the sofas, and had sex with him. I know he wasn't fighting her off. He had hoped to have sex with her that evening, but well, just not like that. After she got what she wanted—literally the second it was over—she walked out, and he didn't hear from her again. We only found out all this when I started working at the pub. One of the other girls had tried it on with the pub manager, but it didn't work on him. He was and still is happily married."

Harley perched on a bar stool and pulled Lizzie between his legs, right up close. They ordered some drinks, and he kissed her again. "I, umm," he started, but he unsure of how to say it or even if he should. "I just wanted to say … I meant it. That was my first time."

"I believe you."

"It's just I know how people usually react to my looks, thinking I'm just a player. That's actually why I've never done anything like this. I can't stand all—"

Lizzie interrupted him with a kiss.

"What was that for?" he asked.

36

"To shut you up."

"Mmmm," he moaned. "I'm glad you were my first," he said before kissing her again.

"I was actually worried you might think I'm a slut, given how long we have known each other," Lizzie commented.

"Nope, I definitely don't think that."

They kissed again. When the drinks arrived, they paused to thank the bartender. "You do realise how difficult it is going to be for me to let you go from now on?" Harley asked.

"I'm sure you'll manage once you get to know the real me."

"Not likely." Harley replied as he placed his hand on the nape of her neck. His fingers stroked the back of her head. He pulled her in for a long, meaningful kiss.

"Are we not going to take the drinks over?" Lizzie asked.

"I'm getting my quota of kisses in, so I can let go of you for a few minutes." That made Lizzie smile.

The moment was broken by Luke's hands grasping Harley's shoulders and giving him the typical laddish shake. Both Luke and Harley had the biggest smiles. Harley grabbed him in a headlock and ruffled his hair.

"Pack it in Hars," Luke said.

"So, what happened?" Harley asked in a joking manner, elongating each word.

Luke still hadn't stopped smiling. Lizzie picked up the drinks for her and Meg, leaving Harley and Luke to talk. She sat down next to Meg and they gave each other the biggest smiles. "I need all the details later," Lizzie said.

The guys were on their way back to the table. Harley firmly bumped shoulders with Luke, making Luke stumble a bit and they both laughed. They split off and came on either side of the girls. Harley's hand brushed along Lizzie's shoulders, sending a shiver down her spine. As he sat down, he kept his arm around her. Luke sat down next to Meg and took her hand, linking their fingers. Harley gave Luke a look of disapproval and shook his head. Luke seemed shy.

"Harley, leave him be. He just doesn't want to be too affectionate in front of us," said Lizzie.

Harley just smiled. It was that sexy smile with the one corner of his mouth. He leaned in and whispered, "Wait till we start on the alcohol later. Won't leave her alone then. That'll break the embarrassment!"

"Later?" Lizzie questioned.

"Yep. You're going to join us for dinner, yes?"

"Of course. That would be nice."

Lizzie and Meg took some drinks back to the room. Meg told Lizzie everything that had happened with Luke. "His soft hands and dreamy voice," she started.

"His defined muscles, and to say the least, he is gorgeous," Lizzie jumped in.

Meg blushed. It was what she had wanted to say, but even to her best friend, she was too embarrassed. They had discussed everything from school and work to hobbies and other activities. They seemed to have loads in common; their university courses were even about animals. Luke was going to be a vet, and Meg was studying so she could go into wildlife rehabilitation.

Luke seemed sweet. They had played a couple of games of pool, had a few more drinks, and then Luke made his move. Meg told how he seemed nervous, but she was just as nervous. During the games of pool, he seemed to be tentatively taking the cue from her in such a way that they got very close. They had brushed arms several times, and at one point, he held her hand. The next time he went to take the cue, he grasped her hand, placed his other hand on her cheek, and softly kissed her on the lips, it had only been a short kiss but enough to break the tension. Meg told Lizzie how she had burst with excitement when he kissed her. And from that point onwards, he hadn't been able to keep his hands off her. At every opportunity he held her hand, put his arm around her, placed his hand on her knee, and kissed her.

Meg seemed really happy. Lizzie was beaming for her friend. "Anyway, enough about me. What happened to you two? You were gone hours."

Lizzie told Meg that she and Harley had very similar taste in music, and they both enjoyed things like tennis and hiking. She told her about the walk along the sand and their first kiss on the beach. Lizzie continued by telling her about him pushing her in the pool. "We wandered around for a while to dry off before we came back to the bar, but then," she hesitated. "Well, we had been getting very close, and we were getting rather carried away. But then he suddenly broke away, saying we should go back to the bar, so he offered to grab me a dry T-shirt. I waited in their lounge, and when he came back with the dry clothes, he kissed me again."

"And?" Meg asked, encouraging Lizzie to continue.

"We got very intimate. Very, very intimate." Lizzie hesitated. "We ended up in his bed, and we had sex."

Meg looked at her with a majorly shocked expression.

"I don't know what it is or why, but I can't control myself around him. He is the only guy I've met who fills me with this uncontrollable need to be with him. He said that I do the same to him."

"It's not even been twenty-four hours, Lizzie."

"I know, I know. But I think I've fallen hard. I don't believe in love at first sight, but … I think I'm starting to change my mind."

"Wow," was all Meg could muster.

"He was lovely though. I had blurted out that it was my first time, and he offered to stop. Then when he went to put on the condom, he gave me the choice to stop again."

"That's nice."

"Strangely, it was his first time too."

"Really, wow. From the looks of him, you wouldn't have thought it."

"No, but he assured me. And afterwards, he even told me that he was glad I was his first."

"Are you glad he was your first?"

"Very much so. I regretted the timing to begin with, with it only being one day, but then in the bar, when he was talking to me, he wouldn't stop kissing or caressing me. It felt wonderful."

"Do you not think he would not have been as intimate with you if you hadn't had sex?"

"Nothing like that. I just get the impression that every time he kissed me or held me before, he was holding back or trying to maintain some level of self-control. When we came back to the bar after, his kisses became softer, more passionate, as if he didn't have to hide or control his feelings anymore."

Lizzie also told her about how when they arrived at the bar, Harley had noticed Luke had made his move and wanted to give them both space. That was why they went to the bar first. "The way Harley spoke about Luke and the way they are with each other, I can tell they are close friends and will always have each other's backs. They are both really great."

While they were talking and getting ready for their dinner with Harley and Luke, there was a knock at the door. Lizzie answered and found the guys standing there, fifteen minutes early, dressed for dinner, and holding drinks in their hands. "Hello. Come in, but I thought we were meeting you at the bar."

"I couldn't wait, so we thought we would bring the drinks to you," Harley said, giving Lizzie a quick kiss on her lips.

Luke smiled shyly. They went in and sat down, putting the drinks down on the central table. Harley was dressed in a casual black shirt with a white pattern on one side and dark denim shorts. The top three buttons of his shirt were unbuttoned, and there lay a steampunk, vintage, broken skull pendant and necklace. His hair was in a similar ruffled spike as earlier. Luke was dressed in a pale but colourful shirt, also with the top few buttons undone, and beige shorts. His hair was neatly brushed in a gentle forwards spike. They looked and smelled gorgeous.

As Harley straightened up, he stepped right into Lizzie. His arms enveloped her, lifting her, and holding her tight. Her legs and arms wrapped around him, and they kissed. He only intended it to be a short kiss, but as he was pulling away, his expression changed. The kiss had sparked something, and they immediately crashed their lips together with a passionate kiss and even tighter embrace. He finished the kiss with a little, quiet "mmm" sound, the type made when eating the most delicious cake or chocolate.

"You look nice," he whispered. He kissed her on the cheek.

Lizzie gave a little embarrassed giggle and smiled. "Thank you."

"Meg, Luke's here. They have brought drinks for us."

Hearing Meg coming through from the bedroom, Luke shuffled over, so there was room for her to sit next to him. His jaw dropped when she appeared. She went to sit next to him, and he told her she looked lovely. Harley told Lizzie that they had been to the bar for a few shots before coming over. Lizzie looked over at Luke and Meg. He had put his arm around her. His other hand was on her knee, and he was leaning right in, giving her a kiss—a long, passionate kiss.

Lizzie was standing, and Harley had perched on the arm of the chair next to her. His arm was still around her waist. He pulled her in closer and kissed her. As he did, he slipped down into the chair using his body to cause her to straddle him. He pulled her in really tight with the one hand on her lower back, clamping her pelvis tight against him. His other hand was running through her hair. Their kiss was using up all the pent-up passion collected during their few hours away from each other. Then they pulled away slightly. He relaxed his tight grip, and they continued talking and kissing for a while. During this time Lizzie commented on how they didn't seem like they were drunk but Harley just responded with a shrug, saying "We aren't big drinkers. It's rare we get drunk. It was just enough to settle Luke's nerves."

Once they finished their drinks, they wandered down for dinner, taking the scenic route. Luke and Meg were holding hands, but Harley was not prepared to let Lizzie go. Every opportunity he had, his arm was wrapped round her or he softly caressed her back, neck or arms. The walk allowed for one such opportunity. His arm was draped over her shoulders, his fingers stroking her upper arm. As they approached the restaurant, they were having to queue, and this gave Harley the perfect opportunity to achieve another embrace and another slow, dreamy kiss.

At dinner, they sat in couples, with Harley and Luke sitting opposite each other. They had a lot of laughs. Harley and Luke talked about when they were trying to book their holiday. They talked about their list of approximately ten different types of holidays, which they just couldn't pick from. They joked about how they ended up scrapping half those ideas when their mum had a massive go at them. Mum's hey, it was all agreed, although with a few of the ideas Lizzie and Meg could see why she was worrying. At one point, though, they confessed that the more dangerous and outrageous ones were more to wind her up. It seemed like they enjoyed winding her up.

Their conversations went on for hours. Harley and Luke talked about what they were like when their parents first got together. At school, Luke was bullied. On the first day, Harley saw Luke being bullied in the playground, and he went over and stood between Luke and the bully, who was a little taller than Harley. Harley was told to move, and when he refused, the bully tried to push him out of the way. Even back then Harley was strong, so it didn't work. When the teachers saw, the bully ended up in trouble. That was the turning point for their friendship. They did almost everything together after that.

The guys continued to tell their stories about school and all the trouble Harley used to get into at primary school.

Harley sounded like he was serious a troublemaker. Luke told them how in senior school, Harley was the one all the girls wanted. "They were literally lining up round the block for a piece of him."

"Piece was right. That's all they wanted, and that was it!" Harley added.

Luke told a couple of the stories and how Harley had never shown any interest in any of those girls. Harley was unusually quiet at this point. He looked embarrassed. He said he just didn't want the type of girl who used to cling to him every chance just to get him to kiss her.

"Like you and Lizzie are today?" Luke joked. Harley kicked him under the table. It was only gently, but it made Luke jump out of shock. He laughed. "No, you're nothing like those desperate girls who were after Harley," Luke said to Lizzie. He turned to Harley and said, "But you have to admit, if you had the chance now, you'd have Lizzie wrapped in your arms, wouldn't you?"

Harley, still looking embarrassed, replied, "You'd be the same with Meg. Admit it."

"Of course. In all seriousness, the girls that Harley tends to attract are desperate. I mean, just look at the disgusting brute," Luke said with a laugh. "Unfortunately for Harley, with him being the *best*-looking guy in school, *all* the girls want him, and *all* guys want to be him. They never just let him be, and that is why he's never had a girlfriend."

Listening to the conversations and banter, Lizzie and Meg were learning lots about Harley and Luke. Luke played the guitar, Harley played the drums, and they were in a band together. They both go for a run every morning, which they even did today. And they both loved cycling and walking.

Lizzie and Meg were rather boring in comparison. They could play some instruments but not well enough to play with their friends in a band. They continued talking about where they lived and what they were doing at university in September. Harley was going into accounting, and Lizzie was training to be a midwife. At this both guys pulled their faces a little. "Rather you than me," Luke said.

Harley laughed but didn't shift his position. His arm remained perfectly still, wrapped around Lizzie's shoulders. She looked up at him, hoping her future profession hadn't put him off. He noticed her gaze and brought his hand up to stroke her cheek. He gave her a kiss.

"Not something I could do, but it's a commendable profession." That made her smile, and she was relieved.

There were not many people left in the restaurant now. The empty tables were being tidied, cleaned and set ready for breakfast. "Oh, wow. We've sat here for hours," Meg commented.

"Right then. To the bar," Luke said.

Harley grabbed Luke, holding him back as they walked to the bar. By the time they all arrived, the guys were deep in conversation. They all stood round the bar and as the drinks arrived Harley announced, "Drinks to the rooms then."

Lizzie and Meg looked at each other and gave each other a sad look. They were upset the night was already over.

Walking back to the rooms, Luke had his free arm wrapped around Meg. He whispered in her ear. Harley caught up with Lizzie, put his free arm around her and said in a strong, confident voice, "You're coming with me."

"See you later," Luke called back while walking Meg towards the girl's room.

Lizzie looked back to Meg, checking she was OK with this, and she smiled back.

In the room, Harley put on some music and then sat next to Lizzie, placing his arm over her shoulders. They sat together, cuddling up and talking about the music. When she finished her drink, he took the glass from her and placed it on the table. As he straightened up, he leaned right into her and kissed her, gently pushing her down so she was lying on the sofa. He lay next to her, leaning right over her. Lizzie's fingers ran over his back and through his hair. He seemed to be enjoying it. His muscles flinched under her touch. His eyes kept closing, and every so often, a soft, breathy moan escaped him.

His free hand caressed her cheek and teased his fingers down her neck. His other arm was underneath the back of her neck; he was using it to support himself. This tenderness continued for ages, just talking and kissing. Their hands running over each other's body, gently caressing and teasing. Eventually they ended up lying together on the sofa, his arm wrapped around her, holding her tight. Lizzie was trapped between the back of the sofa and Harley. With her hand pressed against his chest, she could feel his heart beating and his defined muscles under her fingertips.

At some point they both drifted to sleep. When Harley woke, he carried Lizzie to his bed. When she woke later, Lizzie found herself tucked up cosy at his side. He was lying on his back, his arm wrapped around her. Checking the time, she smiled, only 4 am. She crept quietly to the toilet before cosying back next to him. She placed her arm on him and tickled his chest with her fingers as she drifted back to sleep.

Chapter 5

Second Day

When Lizzie awoke several hours later, she looked up towards Harley. He was awake and had his hand over hers, gently sweeping his thumb over the back of her hand. His other arm was still wrapped around her.

"Good morning, hun. It was lovely waking up with you in my arms this morning," he greeted her.

"Morning, gorgeous. Yes, I definitely like how this feels. When did we end up here?"

"I woke up at some point. It felt cold, so I brought you in here and wrapped us up."

"Thank you."

Harley lowered his head to kiss her forehead before he went to freshen up. He then got drinks while Lizzie used the bathroom. On returning to the bedroom, she saw Harley lying in the centre of the single bed. She placed one leg over him, to climb over. He placed his hands on her hips, manipulating her movements. He was gentle enough that she could resist if she wanted to. He manoeuvred her so she was straddling over his pelvis. She lowered herself, so she was hovering just above him, their bodies parallel. He lifted his shoulders and head to kiss her. He slid one hand up and down her back, while the other slid along her spine until he was tangling his fingers through her hair.

Their breathing was slow and deep, their hearts racing. He pulled her gently against him and kissed her with a deep and intense passion. He stopped and focused on her face before continuing to leave a fiery trail of wet, open-mouthed kisses from one shoulder across to the other, focusing intently on her neck halfway. He unbuttoned her shirt and ran his tongue from her neck down as far as he could reach without moving. Then he retraced his trail with long kisses. The intensity just kept growing. As he reached her lips once again, she stopped him by capturing his lips in a full lock, displaying all her built-up desire. She had pressed her lips against his so firmly his head had sunk into the pillow. Their kissing intensified, becoming rougher and needier.

Harley managed to break her concentration by sliding one hand down her spine, making her back arch from the muscle spasms. His other hand glided from her lips, down between her breasts to hover along the edge of her pants. "Could we have sex?"

Lizzie nodded. His hand descended, his fingers beginning their subtle movements right between her legs before he slid a finger within. The desire Lizzie was experiencing was too much for her, and her pelvis began to rock involuntarily, causing his movements to deepen. His free hand helped to guide the rocking motion, making her movements faster. He could sense her peak nearing. He raised up to a sitting position, and he pulled her hard into him, making Lizzie gasp from the sudden intense fire that movement caused. He clashed their lips together as her body spasms and moans began to erupt from her. His teasing went from soft to firm. Deep motions led instantly to an intense climax. He stopped and did not move for a moment while her whole body pulsated on top of him. Slowly, she regained control of her breathing and of her body. She lay her head on his shoulder, and a breathy moan escaped her as her body relaxed.

Harley flipped them over. Now on top, he took full control. He seductively sucked on her neck while his finger, still within her, began to tease again. With his free hand, he fully stripped her, kissing and caressing her body with his lips before stopping to concentrate some licks between her legs. Her hands came down to try to slow him down, but instead, his free hand clasped them above her head, and his lips dived to her lips, smothering the moans that were trying to break free. His teasing—with his soft, warm lips and his one free hand—increased, and her body moved and clenched uncontrollably. Using his legs, he pinned her down, reducing the amount of movement her hips could achieve. Lizzie's moans increased in intensity and volume. He slammed his lips against hers for a long and powerful kiss. And with a few sudden movements of his fingers, she was, once again, climaxing powerfully. Her whole body was in a rigid contraction. He withdrew his hand slowly, causing her to shudder. He looked at her abdominal muscles that were clenched firmly because of what he had caused, and he showed off his sexy smile.

Harley reached over for a moment. As he positioned himself right over her, he checked if she was still all right. All Lizzie could muster was a nod. He opened the packet in his hand and put on the condom. He lowered his whole body on her, making her shudder. His weight pressing on her heightened the burning desire to feel him deep within her. He brought his lips down to kiss her, and then with one thrust, he was inside. He continued to thrust deeply and firmly. He hadn't stopped kissing her. The passion of the kisses heightening the sensations his pelvic thrusts were causing. The bed's headboard banged against the wall with every thrust.

Lizzie wrapped her legs tightly around his hips, and he groaned loudly. She was starting to reach her peak again. She scratched her nails down his back, causing his body to press firmly into her as his back arched. She wrapped her arms around his shoulders as tightly as she could. Her legs did the same round his hips. The movement sends Harley spiralling to his climax just as Lizzie's hits and they collapse next to each other, completely spent.

Sadly, their after-sex cuddles didn't last long enough. Harley said he needed breakfast. And after checking that everyone was decent, a hesitant Luke walked in. Meg was getting ready and Luke had arranged to meet her for breakfast.

"I'm going to get ready too. See you there?" Lizzie asked. Harley nodded and walked her to the door and gave her the biggest cuddle and a long, lingering kiss on the lips.

"Thank you. I had a great night with you," he said. Lizzie looked up at him and smiled. "See you in a little while for breakfast. And then maybe we can hang out round the pool today."

"I'd like that" she replied.

Harley went back into the bedroom finding Luke stood there with an upset and angry expression. "Hars, it's only the second day of our holiday, and you've already had sex. What the hell?" His voice was stern.

Harley looked slightly embarrassed. "Luke, I'm ..." Harley walked over to the bed and sat down. His head hung low and he ran his hands through his hair. He took and deep breath and exhaled with a sigh.

Luke changed his tone, becoming softer. "Harley, this isn't you. You don't let girls control you like this. It's like she's got under your skin."

"She's not controlling me. But ..." he paused "She has really got to me. I don't think she even realises what she's doing to me."

"What *is* she doing to you?" Luke questioned, rather confused.

"Luke, I feel like I have to be with her. I can't explain it. When I'm not with her, I want to be and when she is here with me, I need to have *all* of her." Harley's voice was soft. He sounded down, like he was still battling with himself.

"Look, I know I lost my virginity badly but it's something special. You've chosen for your first time to be with someone you have *only* just met." Luke sat down next to Harley.

"I know. When you say it like that, it sounds absolutely wrong." Harley sighed. "But Luke, it gets even worse. That wasn't our first time."

"Oh, Harley, what have you done?"

Harley and Luke were more than brothers. They were best friends and they spoke openly about everything.

"Yesterday, after we went for a walk on the beach, I pushed her into the pool. We were meant to be walking back to the bar. We ended up walking round for a while, drying, but it didn't really work. We sat kissing for a while and I felt that I needed more, so I told her we ought to get back to the bar. I knew I wouldn't be able to control myself if we carried on. I kept thinking that it was too soon, but we were both still soaked through, so I went to grab us each one of my T-shirts. Lizzie waited in the lounge, but as I came back from the bedroom, T-shirts in hand, everything was forgotten. I had to have her."

"Geeze mate."

"That's not really the worst of it."

"Oh, Harley." Luke sounded disappointed.

"I asked her to." He stopped not really knowing what to say.

"Harley, you're making this sound really bad. We're here for two weeks. We can't avoid them for that long."

"No, it's not bad. It's just, it was too soon to even have sex and yet I asked her to umm," he started to hesitate again. He took a deep breath and continued, "I asked her to make love to me." He cringed as he said it. Then he started to ramble quickly. "I don't know what happened. I didn't mean to say it. I meant to ask her if she was sure, but oh, I asked that instead."

"Oh, wow. You've got it bad." Luke said with a slight laugh.

"I know. I'm a mess."

Meanwhile, Lizzie and Meg were catching up while changing for the day ahead. Meg told Lizzie how Luke and her kissed and cuddled for ages and eventually cuddled up in her bed before going to sleep. They woke at seven and cuddled and chatted. But by eight their stomachs were rumbling too much, and they decided to get up and get ready. Lizzie told her about Harley. Lizzie couldn't stop smiling the whole time she talked about him and their activities.

"So, you'll be wanting to swap rooms again tonight then?" Meg asked.

"Only if that's what you want also. I don't want to force things between you and Luke."

"I'd like to spend more alone time with Luke," Meg admitted. Just then there was a knock at the door. "Must be the guys. I'll go. You finish getting ready."

Lizzie quickly slipped into her bikini and shorts and came out into the lounge area. Luke was cuddling Meg and giving her a big kiss. "See you've lost your reserve now, Luke. That's good," Lizzie joked.

Harley stood up when Lizzie entered. She noticed his jaw drop a little, even though he tried to hide it. It made her smile and she bit her bottom lip a little.

"You are gorgeous," he said.

"Thank you," replied Lizzie as he locked their lips, commencing a deep and energetic kiss, his arms tightening around her.

Luke slapped Harley on the shoulder, breaking Harley out of his trance. "Shall we go get some breakfast?"

Lizzie had been panicking while walking back to her room. She was worried that she had been too easy, and it might have made Harley think it was just about sex. She didn't want this holiday romance to just be about sex. She really liked him and wanted this to be something she remembered forever. Her worry was over now, though. He still wanted to spend time with her. His kiss was as full of passion just as the kisses were yesterday. That left her feeling giddy and excited.

They all got on so well. It was like they had been friends for years, not just over twenty-four hours. After breakfast they all wandered down to the pool. Lizzie and Meg set themselves up on two sun loungers, settling down to read their books. The guys, who had set up their towels on the loungers next to them, jumped into the pool, splashing the girls' feet.

Later, when the guys got out of the pool, Harley leant over Lizzie, dripping all over her. "Hey, that's not fair. I was lovely and warm," she complained with a smile.

"Well, I can warm you up. Come on. Come for a dip with me." He pulled at her arm.

"You're not going to leave me alone till I say yes, are you?"

"Nope," he replied with his cheeky smile.

Lizzie sighed but then smiled. Harley leant in to give her a kiss. She placed her bookmark and jumped in the water with him. It felt cold at first, but she had been nice and warm in the sun. Harley was underwater and swam right up to Lizzie. He stroked her legs, which made her jump. He trailed his fingers up her legs. Then he kissed her naval before continuing to brush his lips along her body up to her neck. He emerged from the water slowly, still kissing her neck. He wrapped his arms around her waist and she hooked her legs around him. He could stand up in this part of the pool, but Lizzie couldn't. He twisted around so his arms and her back were resting against the wall. He continued to lavish kisses her from her neck, along her cheek, before giving her a long, soft kiss on the lips.

Eventually they went for a swim. They were being silly, doing handstands and seeing how far they could travel underwater. At one point, she dived under the water. He quickly swam under her and facing her, stroked her arms and kissed her. As they resurfaced, he started to tickle her. Then they tickled and tackled each other.

They stayed round the pool till lunchtime, which they all enjoyed together. Harley and Luke went off to play pool at the bar, while Lizzie and Meg went back to the sun loungers. Before settling down to continue reading their books. They enjoyed a swim and talked lots about the books they were reading.

Harley and Luke enjoyed several games of pool before they returned, carrying some drinks for them all. Sitting on the loungers to enjoy their drinks, the guys asked about the books they were reading, and the girls asked who had won at pool. Harley and Luke seemed like they had already had quite a bit to drink. They were a little merry, very talkative, and Luke was being more openly intimate with Meg than he was earlier. It reminded Lizzie of the night before, when Harley told her they had some shots before dinner.

"You're very merry for someone who doesn't drink much?"

Harley smiled. "No, at home we don't drink alcohol very often but we are definitely not teetotal. Because we play in the band we don't drink on stage, so we only tend to drink occasionally. We are on an all-inclusive holiday though, got to take some liberties."

Harley never stopped caressing Lizzie, whether he was tipsy or not. He either stroked her arm, held her hand or wrapped his arms around her. Every time it caused a wave of electricity to sweep through her body. She loved how his touch felt and his attentiveness made her feel special.

When the water basketball game became free, they played a game, girls versus boys. It definitely wasn't a fair game, but the guys weren't trying to win. The game was just an excuse to get keep getting closer to Lizzie and Meg while having fun. Several times they used that to their advantage, Harley kept picking Lizzie up, so she stayed close to the basket. Meg threw her the ball, and Lizzie scored.

Several baskets, cuddles and kisses later, Lizzie and Meg decided they were too far in the lead and swam to the side of the pool. When they turned round, Harley and Luke had disappeared. Suddenly the guys grabbed their feet, making Lizzie and Meg shout out. Harley ran his fingers softly up the outside of Lizzie's legs and over her hips. He held her waist. Like earlier, he started kissing her from her naval to her neck. He seemed to really enjoy what he was doing as his trail of kisses were very slow. He took his time. She was surprised how long he could hold his breath. When he finally got to her lips, he slowly started to pull her under the water. She felt him take a breath. Lizzie took a breath just as her chin was going under the water. Harley was still kissing her. It was an unusual but wonderful sensation to be kissed underwater. The water blocked off every sense except his touch. This sent her body into overdrive.

When they resurfaced to take breaths, she had an overwhelming surge of emotion as she realised just how much she liked him. A tear rolled down her cheek. It was a tear of mixed emotions. She was happy about how she felt but sad that this was going to end when the holiday ended. She was very glad they were in the water as it hid the tear from him. Harley noticed her expression had changed. He knew something was wrong and from his expression he was feeling the same. He placed his hands on her cheeks, cupping her jaw and slowly kissed her. It felt full of passion, devotion and affection. Her entire body, luckily suspended in the water, weakened.

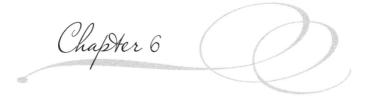

Chapter 6

The Confessions

That evening Lizzie and Meg decided to have dinner alone. They arranged to meet up with Harley and Luke for a few drinks at the bar after. They didn't want to separate from the guys, but Lizzie and Meg needed and wanted some proper girl time. As they were missing out on spending the evening together, they split into couples for the rest of the afternoon. Harley hung out around the pool with Lizzie, and Luke went for a walk along the beach with Meg. It was good, quality, one-to-one time.

On leaving the girls, Harley and Luke went straight to dinner. They had decided to go early and spend the rest of the evening in the bar, playing pool and drinking. It had been what they had intended to do most nights, but then they met the Lizzie and Meg. Luke spoke to Harley about Meg. He was enjoying her company and felt very close to her.

"You're being very reserved with her, Luke," Harley said.

"I know, but I really do like her."

"You had sex with her yet?"

"No," Luke admitted. "But I think she wants to. Last

night we cuddled up in her bed. But we did so much talking that we just ended up falling asleep." Luke was smiling and said again how he really liked Meg and was not about to rush things. He then changed the subject by asking about Lizzie.

Harley sighed. It was a long sigh, a sigh that made Luke realise this was a long, sit-down with a drink kind of conversation. He went over to the bar, collected two drinks and returned the pool cue.

"So, what's happened since this morning then?" Luke asked.

"Nothing's really changed, but I have stopped fighting everything inside."

"And?"

"She's wonderful, amazing and …" He paused and sighed. "Oh, Luke, I'm in trouble. It has only been two days and" Harley rubbed his hand over his eyes and forehead. "Luke, I'm already falling in love her." Harley buried his face in his hands. Luke sat there wide-eyed, speechless and in shock. Harley and Luke usually had deep conversations and they were able to speak openly to each other. But it also helped that Harley was tipsy.

Luke regained himself and placed his hands on Harley's shoulders. "Harley," he paused waiting for Harley to look up "you need to go for it."

Harley sat up, a little shocked. "What?"

"This might only be a holiday romance. Who knows if you will be able to make things work once we are back to normality. When we're back to work, back to our lives. Plus, long-distance relationships can be hard."

Harley was shocked at Luke. This wasn't the type of

thing he expected from Luke, but Harley also agreed with him. "You're right. I'm going to enjoy what I've got for as long as I can. I'm definitely not ready for the 'What happens after holiday?' conversation yet. I think it would devastate me if this is all she wanted. I'd rather save that for the last day."

They finished their drinks. And to change the conversation to a lighter one, they started to play pool again, with more rounds of alcohol.

Lizzie and Meg enjoyed catching up over dinner, just the two of them. It was nice to spend time with each other away from the guys, although they spent most of the time talking about them and their feelings for them. Lizzie admitted to Meg that she was falling hard for Harley. She explained that she felt like she had known him her whole life. They had talked so much and gotten to know each other so well that she felt like she knew everything about him, all their differences and all their similarities. Lizzie realised that wasn't the case as how can you know everything about someone in only a few days?

"I'm just following my gut and enjoying the moments we share. I don't even want to think about what happens when the holiday ends. I don't want to think about this ending," Lizzie said.

They discussed Luke for a while and Meg's feelings for him. It sounded like Meg was really taking a shine to him. Meg gave Lizzie the impression they might actually stay in touch after the holiday. Lizzie wasn't sure what would happen after the holiday between her and Harley. She wanted the relationship to continue but was scared of broaching this subject with him. She wasn't sure if her intense feelings were reciprocated, or even if this was all just intense because of the holiday. For now, she didn't want to spoil what they had. At least nearer to the end of the holiday she expected the relationship to end, and she would cherish the moments they shared on holiday.

After dinner Lizzie and Meg went to the bar. Harley and Luke were still there. They were being loud and rather stupid, but only with each other. They didn't seem to be upsetting anyone else, although luckily the bar was rather quiet. Harley saw them and made an attempt to stagger over. He didn't get very far though, before he collapsed into a chair. They were both laughing so much. As they got closer, Harley just about managed to stop laughing, he stood up and Lizzie realised he wasn't too drunk. He was standing tall and sturdy, with only a little swaying. They were obviously having that much fun and laughing so much it just made it look like he was already drunk from a distance. They were certainly well on their way to being drunk though.

Luke was all touchy-feely with Meg again. He had grabbed her round the waist and planted a firm, affectionate kiss on her lips. Luke and Meg went up to the bar to collect more drinks.

By time they returned, Harley had sat on a sofa and had pulled Lizzie with him. He had manipulated her body so that she was straddling him. He held her tight round the waist, the fingers of his other hand tangled in her hair, pulling her head towards him. He brought her close for a passionate and fervent kiss that didn't stop until they heard Luke and Meg return and put the drinks on the table. Lizzie went to climb off and sit next to Harley, but he tightened his embrace. He wasn't about to let go. Luke and Meg started to play pool, while Harley and Lizzie continued to sit in this embrace and enjoyed their drinks. Harley had one hand round her waist in a tight grip, almost as if she was going to go somewhere if he let go.

He looked up when he placed his empty drink on the table and realised that the pool game was coming to an end. So he suggested they went to get another round of drinks. Luke and Meg returned and sat down. Several drinks and several conversations later, it was time to make a move back to their rooms. They only took drinks of water with them.

On the route to the rooms, Harley stopped, forcing Lizzie to stop as well. There was a tall wall just behind Lizzie and Harley used his body to force her against the wall as he crashed his lips onto hers in a passionate and rough kiss. His emotions were spilling out of him, overwhelming him. Harley still had his arm wrapped around her waist in a tight embrace. He moved his lips, brushing them along her cheek before gently whispering in her ear, "I'm falling in love with you. You're amazing and sweet. Every time I touch or kiss you, I just need you more. I really missed you at dinner."

Lizzie was completely shocked. She hadn't expected it at all. But she was happy. She now knew that he felt the same.

Luke, realising what Harley was telling Lizzie, started to approach, but Meg held him back. "I need to …," he started.

"Go and make sure he doesn't get hurt?" she asked.

"Yeah. He told me earlier how she makes him feel."

"And you're worried she won't feel the same and, therefore, hurt him."

"I just want to protect him. He's just met her and he says he's already falling in love with her." His voice was soft and full of worry for his brother.

"Luke, Lizzie feels the same way about him. She told me earlier too. She didn't use the word 'love', but she did admit she was falling for him, hard." They looked over at the couple. Harley still had Lizzie pinned against the wall, still kissing. "Let's leave them to it," Meg suggested.

Luke, glancing over again, nodded in agreement. "OK."

Just as Luke and Meg were about to walk away, Harley let Lizzie up for air. "Have a good time," Luke shouted back to Harley. "Don't do anything I wouldn't."

"Ha! Ha! Too late for that, Luke. You need to catch up with us." Harley was only joking. He had the biggest smile on his face and Luke smiled back.

"Night, Lizzie," Meg called back.

"Night, Meg. Have fun!" Lizzie responded.

This time Harley and Lizzie went back to the girls' room, while Luke and Meg went to the guys' room. Lizzie put some music on in the bedroom and they lay on her bed. They spent ages talking and just caressing each other. The first subject she broached was what he had just said to her and how she felt about him. It would seem they had a lot to talk about on this subject. The fact that Harley was slightly drunk meant he was more inclined to open up to her, but he wasn't so drunk that he was slurring or falling asleep.

"Harley, did you mean what you just said to me?" she questioned hesitantly.

He brought his hand up to cup her cheek. He leant in, planting a long, soft, affectionate kiss on her lips. "Yes, I'm falling in love with you, Lizzie. Being away from you, even for that short time and talking to Luke made me realise."

"I'm falling in love with you, Harley." They shared another slow, loving kiss. Then Lizzie plucked up the courage to ask what she had wanted to for a while now. She took a deep breath to steady herself. It was visible she was nervous. "So, umm, what next?"

He knew from previous conversations that she was going to university on the south coast of England and for the first time he told her where he was going. He hadn't wanted to say anything before, in case his feelings were deeper than hers. He was only going to be an hour's drive away from her. Lizzie's heart leapt, like it did on the plane the first time she saw his sexy smile.

"Does that mean you'd like to see me again after this holiday?" she asked.

"Of course. I didn't say all that so we could just have a holiday romance." Lizzie was speechless.

Harley had been lying on his side, holding up his head with his arm. Lizzie was lying on her back, right next to him. His free hand had been resting on her stomach, and now he was sliding his fingers up her chest and neck before lightly running them over her cheek. Their eyes fixed on each other, they felt at complete ease, like there was nothing else that needed to be said. He leaned down and kissed her. She started to undo his shirt. She ran her fingers down his chest and stomach, and then along the top of his trousers around to his sides. Lizzie dragged her nails back along the same path before starting to undo his belt buckle. He undid the zip down the back of her dress. She stood to let it drop off her as he removed his shorts. Crawling in bed, he pulled her down, so she was lying on top of him. They remained in close embrace, softly kissing with all the passion they felt for each other, before eventually falling asleep.

Chapter 7

First Dates

When Harley woke, he moved so that he could lean over her. He kept kissing and stroking her until she awoke, at which point he fervently kissed her. He moved so his body was over her. He held her in a passionate embrace and kept gliding his body slowly but firmly against her. He was still kissing her, and his tongue danced intimately round her mouth. His hands left her body for a few moments. She knew he was reaching for protection, but he didn't stop to look at what he was doing. Once it was on, he ran his fingers down the outside of her thighs. Reaching her knees, he pulled them up around him, positioning her right where he needed her. Still maintaining his connection with her lips, one hand returned to weaving through her hair, while his other hand sensitively caressed her waist and hip. He glided up her body, pressing himself firmly against her as he smoothly and slowly penetrated her. He maintained this slow, smooth rhythm, gliding himself against her body.

This felt different from the last times. It wasn't about sex this time, or pleasuring each other. It was deep, slow, sensual and very satisfying. His whole firm, muscular form was gently forcing itself into her entire body. For Lizzie, it ignited a fire within which spread throughout her entire body. The more movements he did the more engulfed she became. She pushed his elbows outwards so more of his weight was against her. Her hands were trailing around his back and through his hair. He was as close to his peak as she was; they could both tell. Their breathing was heavy and strained with the desire to stay in the moment. Throughout, their moans had been breathy and quiet. But eventually, Lizzie could not take anymore. She let out a louder, satisfied moan as she surrendered to the power of her climax, tipping Harley over the edge too. Harley's muscles pulsed so strongly that he was momentarily frozen in position.

They were still kissing, swallowing each other's moans and grunts as the waves of pleasure tried to escape throughout the whole emotional roller coaster. A good few minutes later, Harley regained some control of his body as his muscles had begun to relax. He collapsed face first into the pillow to the side of Lizzie. His arm and leg on one side remained draped over her.

They both needed time to catch their breaths. Finally, they turned on to their sides and faced each other. He was clinging to her like she was going to run away. He had held her like that since last night in the bar. Lying there in a comfortable embrace, he admitted, "I meant everything I said last night by the way."

"I know and so did I."

"Good. I just didn't want you to think it was the drink talking."

"I don't. But the drink did let your protective wall down and that gave me the courage to tell you how I felt too."

He smiled at her. "I enjoyed making love to you. It felt phenomenal."

That made her beam. The moment really was phenomenal. "Me too."

That day they all met up for breakfast again before splitting off for the day, agreeing to meet for dinner and drinks. Although after breakfast, Harley and Lizzie had a difficult time saying bye. They embraced in their tightest cuddle. It felt like they wouldn't be able to release. With how intense Harley had been holding her since last night and how they had admitted their feelings, she suspected that Harley could be feeling worried about losing her. After all, that was exactly how she was feeling. Lizzie gave him a long-drawn-out kiss followed by a whisper in his ear, "I don't want to leave your cuddles, but how am I going to talk about you to my friend if you're still wrapped around me?" It made him laugh and his grip loosened a little.

"I'm all yours tonight again. I promise," Lizzie said with a little smile. Harley smiled, gave her another kiss before he reluctantly released her. He looked sad that he wasn't going to spend the day with her, but he did want to spend time with Luke, tell him all about Lizzie and find out about how things went with Meg.

Lizzie and Meg went to the beach for the morning. They sat talking, catching up on recent events. "Harley was looking at you very intensely at breakfast. What happened last night?"

Lizzie told her everything they talked about last night. Meg looked very happy that they were going to be able to continue the relationship. She knew how much Lizzie wanted that.

"What happened between you and Luke last night?" Lizzie asked.

Meg smiled. "It was great."

"Did you two have sex then?"

Meg gave Lizzie an embarrassed smile which Lizzie knew meant yes. "How was it?"

It wasn't Meg's first time, but it was her first time in years. Meg had ended up regretting her first time and from that point onwards, she never let anyone make her feel that way again. In fact, she hadn't let anyone get that close to her since then. Until Luke. Her experience was what made Lizzie decide to wait for someone who made her feel wonderful. For Lizzie, Harley had been that person and Luke made Meg feel the same way. Unfortunately for them, they were not going to university anywhere near each other and the relationship was going to have to be very long distance for now. But they had already discussed the "What next?" before last night happened. Meg told Lizzie they realised it wasn't going to be easy so they were going to make sure they made the most of this holiday and their time before university started. They knew once university started, things would get more difficult for them both. But they believed their feelings for each other were strong enough. Lizzie knew they would do what it took to stay together. She was very happy for Meg.

With this break from the guys, they managed to finish their books. They had started them on the plane but had spent so long with Harley and Luke, or talking to each other, that they had not had enough time to read. Neither of them complained about that, though. They were too busy enjoying themselves.

Lizzie and Meg enjoyed lunch to themselves. It was very possible that this was the most time they had spent just the two of them during the holiday. They were having a good time, but they also missed the guys. They went back to their room to change out of their sand-covered clothes as they had decided to stay around the pool for the afternoon.

On the way to the pool, the guys had seen them. Harley and Luke sneaked up behind them and tickled their waists. They both jumped and let out almighty screams. But they all had a good laugh about it once the girls realised it was them. Harley and Luke had spent the morning around the pool, taking part in the organised water polo games. They had been for lunch and were just on their way back to the pool after their game of pool. There were two free sun loungers next to Harley's and Luke's that Lizzie and Meg settled on. Lizzie had just laid down, getting comfy, ready to start her new book when Harley came over and sat next to her. He gave her a kiss. "I've missed you this morning," he whispered.

"I've missed you too. Hope you have had a good time though."

"Yeah, Luke and I joined in with the water polo, volleyball and a few other organised pool games. And we talked about you and Meg. He really likes her. It's nice to see him so happy."

"The same goes for her too. We spent a lot of time talking about you two, catching up on what we had missed. Oh, and I finally managed to finish my book without your distractions," Lizzie said laughing.

"You managed to finish it. We've not been distracting you too much then."

"Oh, I don't know," she replied smiling. "I would have finished the second book by now if it wasn't for your gorgeous distractions."

Lizzie felt a little awkward as she realised that she had probably been a little too honest with him. But he just smiled and she felt comfortable again. She was so surprised at how natural their relationship felt and yet it had not even been half a week. When she thought about it, she was concerned things were being rushed, but it really didn't feel wrong or rushed. It helped being on holiday and, therefore, being able to spend every moment together if they wanted. If they had been at home—back to reality, working and seeing other friends—these last few days would have been most likely spaced out over a few weeks. On holiday they only had to concern themselves with mealtimes. If they missed the restaurant schedule, they might miss a meal, and Harley and Luke definitely would not have coped with that. The holiday and time they were able to spend together meant they got to know each other really well. They felt comfortable enough to tell each other anything and everything. There was no awkwardness, no worry about saying something wrong or sounding stupid. They could just be themselves. They could be honest and they trusted each other wholeheartedly.

Lizzie and Meg continued to read their second books of the holiday and the guys went to partake in the organised pool sports for the next hour. A soaking wet Harley arrived back, leaned over and kissed Lizzie, dripping all over her.

"Thanks," she said, wiping her face dry. He just flashed that cute smile of his. It still made her shiver all over.

They ended up staying together for the rest of the afternoon before splitting off to their own rooms to get changed for dinner. "Oh, by the way, we have booked us tables at the Panorama Bistro," announced Luke.

Harley and Luke beamed at Lizzie's and Meg's shocked expressions. Meg started to say something, but Harley cut her off. "We will bring drinks to your room in an hour, give you two chance to get ready." Then the guys walked off, not giving the girls a chance to answer.

The girls looked at each other, still with the shocked expression on their faces. They knew this restaurant did table service. Then they suddenly realised they only had an hour. They picked up their things and ran back to the room as fast as they could. They had a lot to do to make sure they were ready for a nice restaurant. The complex's main restaurant was nice, but this was one of the posher ones. Lizzie and Meg needed showers; they needed to wash their hair. They wanted to make sure they were dressed to impress. Meg had decided to wear her baby-blue, satin wrap long flowing dress. Lizzie wore a deep red, off-shoulder wrap dress.

An hour later, Harley and Luke arrived with drinks. They brought Lizzie and Meg elaborate cocktails with straws, which they enjoyed on the way to the restaurant. As they arrived at the restaurant they were split into couples.

"We thought you might like a date night for a change. You really do look gorgeous," Harley told Lizzie.

"That sounds lovely. And thank you." He had told her she looked gorgeous back in the room, but it was still nice to hear it again.

Harley and Luke had asked the restaurant to ensure the two tables were completely separate and the restaurant had sat them at opposite ends. Harley and Lizzie still seemed to have loads to talk about. The recent development of continuing the relationship after the holiday and the fact that their universities were not too far from each other gave them even more to discuss. They talked about things they could do together when they were back in England and they got to know their hobbies, similarities and dislikes. Although they had discussed some of these things before, there was more meaning this time, so more detail was expressed and a lot more questions asked. This knowledge would contribute to each other's lives from now on. They were no longer two individuals on holiday, enjoying their holiday romance. They were a couple, and their lives would be interlinked for the foreseeable future.

Harley told her all about the pub he worked at and the mates he made there. He discussed what they were like—warning her was probably more like it though, as they were all loud and outspoken. He asked about her work and friends. She told him that she struggled to fit in at school, but that two years ago she was offered to assist at a holiday club and it spiralled from there. After holiday she would be working there until she went to university. Her manager had even asked her if she would like to return during university holidays. Lizzie said she loved working there. She never had time to be bored as the kids always wanted to be entertained. Plus, she had become good friends with some of her colleagues.

Lizzie and Harley discussed movies they liked and ones that were coming out soon that they wanted to watch. They talked about going to the cinema and on walks or bike rides. Harley joked about teaching Lizzie to play the drums. Lizzie asked him if he would have a go at horse riding. She wasn't a good rider, but she enjoyed going to places that did horse trekking.

It was a very romantic candlelit dinner. They held hands and played footsy under the table. Lizzie felt so special. He ordered sparkling wine and they enjoyed a delicious starter and main course. When they reached dessert, they ordered two so they could share. One of them was chocolate mousse. When it arrived, Harley took a little of it on his fork and leaned over, placing it to her lips. Lizzie was biting her bottom lip but stopped so she could accept the food. They shared a little laugh. It was a cheesy move, but it felt good. They ate the desserts, finished the sparkling wine and continued to talk for ages.

Eventually, the restaurant was closing, and they were asked to leave. Luke and Meg were also being asked to leave. Joining them at the door, they all went to the bar. Lizzie linked arms with Meg and they shared giddy little giggles while commenting on how amazing the restaurant was, how delicious the food was and to top it off, how wonderful the company had been. They were both starting to feel the effects of the alcohol, but they were also incredibly happy.

Lizzie and Meg walked a lot slower than the guys and by time they reached the bar, Harley and Luke had organised another bottle of sparkling wine and chosen a table tucked in a dark corner, out of the way of everyone. The table had two sofas. Harley was sitting on one, and Luke was on the other. They had already poured the drinks. Harley raised his glass towards Lizzie and they clinked in a toast. "To us," he said. Lizzie gave a little shy smile. Then they all made a toast, "To the holiday."

Harley reached his arm round Lizzie's shoulders and

pulled her close. Lizzie got comfortable and with her free hand, reached up to his face. She turned his head towards her and kissed him. "Thank you for tonight. It's been really lovely," she said.

"You're worth it."

"You're too good to be true," she said with a laugh.

"What? I'm just trying to show you how much you mean to me."

"You're spoiling me. Anyway, I already know how you feel about me. You told me last night and you've shown me every day."

"And now I'm showing you today."

The music changed to a song Harley and Lizzie both liked. "Dance with me?" he asked.

"Of course."

He stood up and held out his hand to her. He was really going all out, trying his best to be a proper gentleman on this date. He led her to the dance floor and twirling her round, he brought her right in. He surprised her; he actually knew how to dance properly, actual ballroom-style dancing. He led her round the floor smoothly to a rock and roll. His lead was seamless and although Lizzie didn't know the moves, his lead meant it didn't matter too much. Lizzie asked him how he knew this dance. He told her all about his mum taking him for ballroom and Latin dance classes when he was a child. It was one of the things his dad had hated him doing. "Mum even got Luke enrolled for a while."

"When did you stop?"

"Oh, we were about ten or eleven, just before we started senior school. Although", he continued "I'm not holding you properly. If I was in my class, I wouldn't be quite so close to you, and we would need to have a rather ridged frame."

"You keep surprising me." Once again, he had shown another side to himself. It was also the first time he mentioned his dad, but Lizzie decided it was not the right time to ask him about that.

When the song finished, the DJ played "Lady in Red" by Chris De Burgh and Harley led Lizzie in a different dance. "What is this one?" she asked.

"The rumba. But don't worry. We will stick with the basics." He pulled her in as close as he could. He leaned over and gave her a kiss. During the song he whispered, "I want to make love to you tonight, my lovely lady in red." This really was a magical night.

Lizzie was not able to reply. It was as if she had lost all control over her voice. He started to stroke her back and lavish kisses on her neck. His kisses were becoming fiercer, more intense. He gently started to suck and nibble at her neck. He was making her body feel like it was on fire.

"I'm going to tease you" he continued, showering her with kisses every few words, "so much from now until we get back to the room that you'll be begging me to take you. I want your emotions, your passions so high that when I get you into bed, my kisses will feel like explosions." He couldn't see her face, but he could feel the effect he was having on her body. Her breathing had deepened, her heart was racing; he had her exactly where he wanted her.

Harley and Lizzie went back to the table and drank the rest of the wine. He continued to glide his fingers over her arms, her hands and through her hair. He was endlessly trailing kisses along her neck, cheek and lips. His soft, succulent lips only left her skin when he stopped to drink. At one point he took a sip of his sparkling wine and kissed her neck. The bubbles from the wine tingled her neck and some of the wine ran down her back, leaving a bubbly, wet trail. He kissed her lips again.

Lizzie really wanted him now. Her hands started to feel under his untucked shirt. She ran her nails along his stomach from side to side, causing him to stop kissing her for a moment. The sensation caused a shiver to take over his body and a breathy moan escaped his lips.

"You trying to get your own back?"

"Just expressing how you're making me feel," Lizzie said, biting her lip as he ran his fingers down her spine.

"Come on. Let's go," he said. She bit her lip again, took his hand and stood up.

"See you two lovebirds in the morning," Luke said.

Luke and Meg had been sitting cuddled up close the whole time. They had been talking, kissing and caressing, but now they stood up too. Harley spoke to Luke for half the walk back to the rooms. Harley then wrapped his arm around Lizzie, sweeping her round to make her stop right in front of him. He kissed her.

"You did all that just to get a kiss?" Lizzie joked.

As Harley and Lizzie reached the room, he used his body to press her back against the door. He swept his lips along her neck until her breathing deepened again. She slipped her hand down his body. Reaching his belt, he paused and pulled away from her.

"Careful, or I might have to take you right here, right now."

"You best hurry and get me to your room then."

He walked her in, directing her footing as she travelled backwards. She was unbuttoning his dark grey shirt as he was unzipping her dress. The second the door shut behind them, Lizzie's dress fell to the floor, along with all his clothes. He effortlessly lifted her. Lizzie squeezed her legs round him while he carried her to bed. He was still tantalising her skin with his touch and his fiery kisses, which he lavished everywhere, as he gently lowered her on to the bed. Climbing on top, he brought their lips together, so they were just about brushing together. Lizzie's heart was racing, and she repeatedly raised herself to attempt a kiss, that he prevented. On about her tenth attempt, he turned her onto her front. Her body shivered as his wet tongue skated down her spine, followed by gradually and gently blowing a cool breeze over the same path. He pinned her arms down at her sides, preventing her from turning over until he had teased her spine several times. This time when she tried, he let go, allowing her to turn under him. From her expression, he could tell she wanted him, which made him smile his cute, sexy smile. Reaching for protection, she drew her nails down his tensing abdominal muscles, making his body flex further.

"You're not allowed to tease me back, you know."

"Really? You didn't say that earlier."

He seized her wrists with one hand and pinned them above her head. He put on the protection and then, with his free hand, manoeuvred her knees as his pelvis slid forcefully against hers. She could feel he was ready, just as she was. But Harley just smiled and continued to tease. Their bodies slid together, their hips colliding. It was getting too much for Lizzie to bare. Yet he continued to lay his fiery trail of open-mouthed kisses on her exposed skin.

"Please, Harley" she begged in a breathy moan, but he only smiled and began to succulently suck on her neck and continued to caress her body with his free hand.

"Harley, please. Please make love to me now." Between each word she had to take a breath as he had heightened her emotions so much. Now she was breathless and wanting.

As she said the word "now" he let himself enter, causing the word to become distorted by a satisfied moan. A breathy sigh escaped Harley too. He brought his lips to collide with hers with a passionate and vigorous kiss. Their bodies synchronised, pulsing together as waves of emotions tore through them. Lizzie's legs were wrapped tightly around his waist, deepening their connection. Their lips were in a tight lock, trying to capture the satisfied moans and breathy sighs which filled the room. They were lost deep within each other as they climaxed before collapsing down, all their energy expelled.

They cuddled up, their legs tangled, and his arms enveloping her close and tight. She buried her head into him, feeling his wonderfully formed naked muscles firmly against her.

"Goodnight, hun," he said as he landed a kiss on her forehead.

"Goodnight, gorgeous."

Then they drifted to sleep.

Chapter 8

The Unintentional

Harley woke to find Lizzie stilled wrapped up in his arms, their legs still tangled. Her cheek was pressed against his muscular chest. He softly weaved his fingers through her hair. He had a sudden pulse, a strong urge. His muscles contracted as he realised he was actually in love with her. He tried to deepen his breathing, trying to control the urge to say it out loud. But it was too late. He had already said it. He had whispered, "I love you, Lizzie."

Every part of him froze. Holding his breath, he hoped she was still asleep and hadn't heard him. His mind was racing; it was too soon. It was bad enough he had admitted he was falling for her, but now? All he could do now was hope that she hadn't heard.

A few moments later, she stirred, arching her back slightly so she could make eye contact. "Good morning, gorgeous."

"Good morning, hun." He was as controlled as he could be despite being full of worry. Lizzie went to freshen up in the bathroom. Lying on the bed alone, he breathed a sigh of relief. His mind was still racing. It was too early to feel these feelings and definitely too early to announce them. His hands stroked over his face, thankful that she had not heard him.

Harley freshened up too, and then poured them both a glass of water, which they drank as he perched on the side of the bed. Climbing back into bed, he went to cuddle up next to her, but she had different ideas. As he leant in to give her a kiss, she moved. As he came further forward, she swiftly rolled onto his back. Holding his arms down by his side and putting all her weight on his hips. She started to get him back for last night. She ran her tongue down his back, exhaling a cool breeze as she rose back to his neck. Once there, she succulently sucked and she gently bit. His moan told her he had enjoyed that, so she bit him slightly harder. His groan deepened.

Harley's body was randomly twitching as he succumbed to the sensations her touches were causing to stir within. His muscles contracted sharply. He tried to turn, but she had been expecting him to try, so her secure grasp won, this time. She continued to repeat her teasing over and over, down his spine and at his neck, until he couldn't take anymore. He flipped over, ensuring he grabbed hold of her so she wasn't thrown off balance and fall off the single bed.

Lizzie bit and licked her bottom lip, before placing it right next to his lips. She wanted to tease him like he had teased her last night. As she pulled away from his kiss, he smiled. "You trying to get me back for last night?"

"Of course. Fair is fair."

"You think you can?"

"Oh, I already am."

"Mm, true." He couldn't deny it. His body was pulsating with desire under her, and he was already wanting more.

Then she brushed his lips again with hers, and interlinking their fingers, she pressed his hands into the bed. She shuffled down slightly to kiss his neck. His breathing had changed slightly, but not enough. She ran her tongue over his chest, circling his nipples and ran her teeth and tongue as low down his stomach as she could reach. She could see the effect this was having as his muscles contracted erratically. She came back to brush her lips against his. He tried to come up to kiss her, but she moved away again. He was biting his lip, his breathing had intensified now, getting deeper and slower. His body pulsated and clenched under her. His facial expression was of pure pleasure and bliss. She lit his skin on fire as she trailed her wet lips down to his neck and bit, firmly, making him suddenly gasped. She looked up at him but wasn't able to tell if his expression was of pain or pleasure. She bit him again with the same vigour, watching his face this time for clues. He gasped. His face scrunched slightly but then relaxed as he exhaled with a long moan. She continued her teasing trail over his exposed skin. His body movements were getting stronger. She didn't know how much longer he was going to let her hold him in position. This was going to be her only opportunity. She slowly ascended his body, continuing to trail her wet lips along his skin. As she reached his lips, Lizzie hoovered just above and made eye contact. "I love you, too, Harley," she whispered.

His face changed to shock before his affection for her burst out.

He sat up, grasping her into a tight embrace and slowly,

passionately, affectionately kissed her. All their feelings for each other poured out in this long, sensuous kiss. He lay her down next to him. They were already lost within the moment and everything around them just seemed to disappear. They continued to kiss, with soft, tender, deep kisses. They locked eyes as he stroked along her cheek. She could see the depth of his affection and devotion in his expression. He closed his eyes and kissed her passionately as their bodies merged in synchronised waves. Their movements were slow but forceful, pressing their entire bodies together. He turned her so he was lying on top of her, his body weight pressed on her as she pushed his elbows outward. Their bodies were being forced against each other, yet it still wasn't close enough. They were perfectly aligned, and she could feel him pulsing with her. They were filled with the desire and love they felt for each other. Their lips caressed each other's lips and tongues. Their bodies were displaying it with force. They were wound around each other. Their arms and legs wrapped securely and tightening as they shared the need for deeper motions. Gentle, breathy moans and deep breathing filled the room. The sounds weren't escaping them as their lips were still sharing in their pleasure.

A faint knock sounded at the bedroom door, but they were consumed. They had no recollection of their surroundings. Their bodies filled with intense desire, like they were on fire as Lizzie began to climax. Harley was still muffling any sounds she might make with kisses as he picked up speed and force, getting very close himself.

A knock sounded again, this time slightly louder. Luke, standing on the other side of the door, could hear none of what was going on. He assumed they must be asleep and started to open the door as quietly as he could. At which point he saw them. "Oh, Harley, you could have at least told me to piss off," he said sharply.

Harley suddenly stopped. He raised his body off Lizzie, like he was doing a press-up, but it was too late for him to say anything. His climax hit that exact second and he dropped to the bed. He buried his head in the pillow, trying to muffle the grunts escaping him as his body was vigorously pulsating.

"Sorry, Luke. We didn't hear you," Lizzie said.

"Oh, well, I was just popping by to change, I'll just come back after breakfast."

Harley didn't move. He couldn't do anything until his body began to relax. Lizzie looked at him. "Are you OK? That one seemed to be more intense."

"You need to grab yourself a T-shirt." His voice muffled by the pillow.

Lizzie grabbed one of his T-shirts and put it on. "What is it, Harley? You don't seem as happy as I thought you would be after that wonderful session."

Harley was sitting up ensuring the sheet was discretely covering him. "Lizzie," he started, patting the bed next to him, "I'm sorry." He looked distraught.

Lizzie was confused. "What for? That was wonderful."

"I hadn't put any protection on."

"So, I presume the bed's all wet then," Lizzie joked.

"Yes, but Lizzie," he hesitated a moment. "It's only because Luke entered that it's on the bed."

"Yeah," Lizzie said and sighed.

"I don't know what happened. We've used a condom

every time." Harley sat up, took a deep breath and rubbed his hands over his face.

"Let's just be thankful it is on the bed," she said.

There was a lengthy pause, neither of them really knowing what to say. They sat there for a short while, side by side. Harley took a deep breath. "I'm sorry," Harley said to her. "I don't know what happened. We haven't forgotten before."

"It was just as much my fault. If I hadn't been so deep into my feelings or teased you for so long, I might have realised."

"I know it's not nice that Luke walked in, but it's a good thing he did. That was far too close."

"Yes, a good thing we were interrupted. Otherwise, I might have had a big belly in my not-too-distant future."

Harley paused and sighed. He stroked along her jaw. "Just so you know," he said as he lifted her chin so he could make eye contact, "I wouldn't have left you alone if that had happened."

That made her smile. He kissed her and again apologised for the unintentional mistake.

He then held her tightly. It felt the same but also different, but Lizzie couldn't determine what about it felt different. She decided to put it down to what just happened and the fact that she felt a little awkward about not stopping things and knowing he probably felt the same.

Harley gave her a kiss on the forehead. "Join me for a shower?"

"Umm, yes please." Lizzie replied.

Harley grabbed the body wash and lathered them both

up. "I'm going to smell as good as you today," she joked with a big smile.

Harley just smiled. He would have usually laughed at such a silly thing, but he seemed on edge. He had deliberately been making contact since they got out of bed, sometimes with little touches here and there, and other times he held her hand or placed his hand on the small of her back.

After they were dressed, he kissed her. He took her hand as they left the room to go for breakfast. During breakfast she noticed that they only spent a few minutes not holding hands or without his arm wrapped around her. He was also quieter than normal. She had the distinct impression he didn't wanted to leave her alone because of what happened. He still seemed really nervous and continuously apologised, despite her telling him it was her fault also, and he didn't need to apologise anymore.

She realised they needed to talk as this morning's mistake was obviously still weighing heavily on his mind. "Let's go back to the room," Lizzie said after breakfast.

"Why? Is everything OK?" he asked, his voice full of panic and a wide-eyed worried expression on his face.

"Yes, but I need to get changed. I'm still dressed in last night's clothes."

"Oh, yes." It was the first time he had properly smiled, He seemed to have relaxed a little.

They bumped into Luke and Meg on the way back to the room. Lizzie stopped to ask Meg if they could have the room for a while without interruption. She had a rather serious look on her face.

"Of course. Is everything all right?" she asked.

"Yes. I promise I will fill you in later."

Back in her room, Lizzie got changed, Harley sat on her bed, waiting. He still looked agitated and worried. His hands were constantly rubbing together or fidgeting. Lizzie went into the lounge area and poured two waters. Harley followed her, so she sat on the sofa. Now that he saw her sat waiting for him, he started pacing. His hands were rubbing through his hair, and it was clear that he felt burdened.

"You're breaking this off, aren't you?" he asked abruptly. He looked so nervous. "I mean, I don't blame you. Who has sex without making sure they are wearing protection. And to top it all off, I caused it by stupidly blurting out my feelings for you. How stupid am I for saying that sort of thing after only a few days?"

Harley was rambling, and Lizzie was trying, unsuccessfully, to get a word in. In the end she stood up, stopped in front of him and took his hands. "No. No, not at all. I meant it when I told you I love you, and I still mean it," she said calmly and clearly.

He breathed a sigh of relief, calmed down a bit. He sat down with her. "What did you want to talk to me about then?"

"You." Lizzie remarked.

Chapter 9

Harley's Past

"You seem nervous about something, and it seems to be weighing on you ever since our, umm" she paused again, trying to think of the right word, "mistake." Another deep sigh and he went really quiet and hung his head low. All Lizzie could think of was that he had lied to her about something. Everything went quiet.

"Holiday is not really the time to talk about this. And it's certainly not the type of conversation that you have on the fourth day of a relationship. But I suppose with our relationship and the way that I feel about you, it's different. I want this to continue for ..." He trailed off, exhaling sharply.

Lizzie just sat in silence, she thought it best just to let him do the talking and open up when he was ready. She was worried that if she said anything, he would close up again, causing strain on them both.

"I ... I can't express my feelings for you very well. I've never felt like this about anyone before and now ... now I feel like I'm about to ruin it. I thought what happened earlier would have ruined how you felt about me but it also," he took a deep breath and paused for a moment, "it also made me remember something that happened quite some time ago. That's why I went so quiet. Trouble is, I'm now worried about telling you in case that changes the way you feel about me." His words were quick. He was rambling now, but she understood that the mistake had triggered a hidden feeling or memory that he was having trouble with.

His head still hung low. Lizzie didn't move or say anything.

"It's about my parents and what happened before they split. I was only six when they separated. I don't necessarily know the truth; I just know what I experienced and heard. I think it started slowly as Mum said it had got progressively worse over about six months. To begin with, he just used to get drunk. Then about three months into that, he lost his job. That's when it all got bad."

Harley was taking it slowly. He had to take deep breaths regularly, and he clenched, rubbed and fidgeted with his hands.

"Dad started to get drunk every night. From what Mum has told me, he started hitting her. She threatened to leave him if he didn't get himself straight, but it just continued to get worse. For the last month or so, when he got home, he used to come up to my room first. He used to check that I was sleeping, and if I wasn't, he either slapped me round the head, or when he was in a very bad mood, hit me on the back, sometimes winding me. Trouble was, he was always so noisy when he came through the front door, he used to wake me up. No matter how much I tried to look like I was sleeping, it didn't work. Sometimes he used to throw my bedroom door open so harshly it banged and made me jump. Then I would hear him and Mum. He used to force her to have sex with him, and if she refused, I heard him hitting her. Things got smashed a lot."

Harley was still concentrating his gaze to the floor. His hands still clenched. "He hit her for lots of reasons, but that's not the important bit for now. One night it was the worst I had heard it. He was in a horrifyingly monstrous mood. He blasted through the front door. I remember grabbing a pillow to put behind me, but this time he didn't come into my room. I heard him shouting at Mum, and then I heard what I thought was a muffled scream and lots of regular bangs. I later learnt it was the kitchen table being hammered against the wall. Mum was not well after that. She couldn't even walk me to school without taking painkillers. I don't think she realised I knew that. A few weeks later, Mum started to become ill."

While he paused to gather his thoughts, Lizzie grabbed a box of tissues. Even if he didn't need them, she did. She placed her hand on his knee. He sat up and took a sip of his drink. As he looked up, he noticed that she had been crying, and that caused him to let his pent-up emotions show. Tears formed in his eyes. He cuddled up to her and they sat in silence for a moment before relaxing, still cuddling. As he continued, he spoke through his tears, but he was more relaxed now. Harley realised that he had already said the hardest part and Lizzie hadn't run out screaming or told him to leave. So, he felt comfortable to finish his story.

"To begin with, Mum just thought she was unwell. She went to the doctors and eventually found out that he had given her an STD. That afternoon, when she collected me from school, we didn't walk home. Instead, she took me straight to a women's and children centre. She had only taken a few items from home and a couple of days' worth of clothes. She didn't want him getting suspicious too soon. They kept us safe and hidden for a few days, until she went into hospital for her surgery. But she knew I couldn't stay there while she was in hospital and while she was recovering. She arranged with the staff for a foster family to take me in for three months. Her plan was for us to move to a different centre, far enough away that she wouldn't need to worry about him. She chose a foster family carefully and selected one that lived about an hour away. That way she didn't have to worry about me accidentally bumping into him either. That's actually when I first met Luke. His dad was the foster parent who took me in. We don't share that information with others as it leads to too many difficult questions about my past. Our story that we told you originally is what we tell everyone. It's basically the truth. We were thrown together; we just omit the horrible parts and the fact it was through me being fostered."

He looked at Lizzie to see if she was all right. He had just admitted he hadn't exactly told her the truth and was a little worried about that. He could see she still had tears in her eyes.

Lizzie noticed his nervous glance. "Don't worry about that omission. I completely understand why you don't go around saying that truth. Please tell me more."

"Luke and I got on so well while I was with them. I was enrolled at the same school as Luke. That's when I stood up for him against the bully we told you about. I was only meant to be staying with them for three months, but Mum had some complications. It was six months before she was well enough for me to go back to her. By then, Luke and I had a deep, brotherly bond, so his dad continued to let me come round to play. Mum had intended on moving away, so she found a centre nearby. We eventually got a small flat, just the two of us. I went to play at Luke's every weekend. Mum obviously met his dad, and things developed for them from there. When our lease came up for renewal, that's when they decided to move in together.

"It had been just over a year since the incident with Dad, and we had not seen him or heard anything from him. Mum was able to file for divorce during this time, which was great. The only downside to the whole situation meant that she could no longer have children. Not that Harry and Mum wanted anymore, not with Luke and I causing loads of havoc." Harley paused for a moment, giving Lizzie a tight squeeze.

"With us being together without protection earlier, even though I knew we hadn't been with anyone else, I couldn't help but think of Dad giving Mum that infection because he had unprotected sex. And I just started to compare my actions to what he did."

They cuddled for a little while longer. Lizzie was upset by what he and his mum had been through. When she managed to find her voice, she sat up slightly so she could make eye contact. "Harley, from what I know about you, you are nothing like your father, and from the sounds of it, you ended up with a wonderful mother and stepfather who love you and helped mould you into the person you are today. Our little mistake does not make you anything like your biological dad."

Harley breathed a sigh of relief. "I'm actually really glad

I told you. You now know most things about me and that was the worst of my memories."

"I'm glad you told me too. I love you, Harley."

"And I love you." He sat up and freshened himself up. "Could you not tell Meg?" he said hesitantly. "At least for now. I just need to tell Luke. He might want to tell her himself."

"I won't for now. But let me know what he decides. I don't like keeping secrets from Meg, especially ones that affect her, even something this minor for her part."

"I will. When you do talk to Meg, or anyone else about this though, just keep most of the details to yourself. I've told you everything, but if it was anyone else, I would have just said I had a bad father."

"Don't worry. I won't talk to Meg about it until you tell me I can, and I'll keep it short. No details, I promise. I also can't see why I would ever need to tell anyone else any of this." She paused for a moment. "Harley, thank you for telling me everything about it. It must have been hard for you."

Harley leaned in and kissed her. "Surprisingly it wasn't. I think because of how we are together, it felt right telling you. I would have told you eventually. It just shouldn't have come up in the first week. Although the same could be said for a lot of things we have done, said and felt this week." He laughed.

"Right," he continued, "now for some fun. I've had enough serious for one day. Swim?"

Chapter 10

Fun Time

They treated themselves to a cocktail on the walk. Arriving at the pool, they saw Meg and Luke had saved sun loungers for them. Meg looked at Lizzie quizzically. She could tell Lizzie had been crying.

"Everything is great. I will talk to you later about it. I need a bit of fun first," she said before jumping into the pool next to Harley.

They swam for a bit, and Lizzie tried her best to make Harley laugh. He wasn't the easiest person to make laugh, but she usually managed to. Luke and Meg joined them in the pool and they played basketball.

"Girls versus boys?" Luke asked.

Lizzie and Meg looked at each other. "One condition: You play properly," Meg replied.

"OK, but you know that means we will win," Harley said laughing.

"That's OK," both Meg and Lizzie said.

For a while, Harley and Luke made loads of shots, but eventually they started to get mischievous. Harley and Luke started to hold, cuddle, kiss and tickle the girls. The girls didn't complain though, and after Harley's discussions with Lizzie earlier, they both needed to have some fun.

After lunch, Harley held Luke back, walking very slowly. Lizzie turned and saw them deep in conversation. Harley noticed and smiled at her before noting that Lizzie had taken Meg up the path to the tennis courts.

"Just going to book a court," Lizzie shouted back. "See you back at the pool in a bit."

Lizzie kept the conversation light with Meg. She did ask about what happened in the room, but Lizzie just said she would rather talk about it in private later. Meg understood; there were a lot of people around.

Harley told Luke they needed to talk, so they continued walking round. "Where do I start, Luke? I messed up this morning, big time."

"You've got yourself into trouble a lot this holiday, Hars," Luke joked. "So that's why you were acting so strangely earlier then?"

"Yeah. Lizzie was asleep this morning, and I had a sudden feeling come over me. I stupidly said, 'I love you, Lizzie,' out loud. I didn't even realise I said it until it had come out."

"Wow."

"Gets worse."

"You really don't do well with girlfriends, do you?"

"Hey, she still loves me, even after all this."

"She said it back then?"

"Yes," Harley said, a massive smile spreading across his face.

"So, what happened next?"

"We got all caught up in the moment. When you

walked in, oh man, you had the best and worst timing. As you walked in, it made me jump and I instinctively pulled away from Lizzie. But then, literally that second, I shot my load all over the bed."

"Oooo, mate, no condom, or did it fail?" asked Luke with a nervous laugh.

"No condom. I've put one on every time, until this morning."

"Well, I can see why you said best but worst." Luke was still chuckling at Harley's misfortune.

"Yep. If you hadn't walked in at that exact moment, Lizzie and I might have a bundle of joy in nine months rather than going to uni." There was a pause before Harley continued "Well, that all made me think about what happened with Rick, and I started to get quieter. I wasn't comparing the situations, but it did make me re-live the memory. Lizzie realised something was wrong and asked me."

"That's why you went back to her room then?"

"Yeah, I ended up telling her all about Rick and Mum and the fostering. I just wanted to tell you as I figured that you would probably want to tell Meg. I know Lizzie and Meg would want to talk a little about it. She has promised to keep the details to herself, but you know what girls are like, they need to talk things through."

"I'll tell Meg now, get it over with. You don't think Lizzie would have said something already though?"

"No. I asked her if I could talk to you first, in case you wanted to be the person to tell Meg."

"Thank you. Oh gosh, what a discussion for a four-day old relationship."

"At least that's all for you. I've told Lizzie I love her after only four days, told her all about Rick, and to top it all off, I nearly got her pregnant. I hope the rest of the holiday is less exciting." Harley and Luke laughed.

Harley and Luke had walked the long route back to the pool. As they arrived, they wandered over to Lizzie and Meg who were sat reading. Harley sat with Lizzie and told her that he and Luke had a good chat about everything and that he knew Harley had told her everything. Luke had approached Meg and asked her to go for a walk on the beach. Harley said that he was talking to her now. Lizzie was glad as it meant that she could talk to Meg about it later.

When Luke and Meg returned, he and Harley went to play volleyball on the beach. Meg sat next to Lizzie and just looked at her. "You're wondering about this morning?"

Meg just nodded. "Where do I start?" Lizzie took a deep breath. "This morning Harley told that he loves me, and I ended up saying it back."

"Oh wow. I assume you meant it?" Meg asked.

"Completely. But then we ended up completely zoned out as if nothing and no one were around us. We were completely wrapped up with our feelings and were making love when Luke came in. He assumed we were asleep as we hadn't responded to his knocking." Meg looked shocked.

"It gets worse. As Luke walked in we were suddenly dragged out of this," Lizzie shrugged, "bubble, I guess, and we came to realise that we hadn't used any protection. If Luke hadn't walked in when he did …" She trailed off.Meg was just listening intently.

"Harley didn't stop apologising for it. I think he must have apologised about a hundred times before he agreed to stop saying it. It's not like it was just his fault. At one point when we were talking about it, I said that at least it was stopped before it ended up as a big problem."

"What did he say in response to that?"

"He told me he wouldn't have left me alone to cope."

"That's sweet," Meg said with a smile.

"Yes. But he still wouldn't leave me alone. I love all his affection, but it seemed different. As time went on, he seemed to be getting quieter and sadder. That's when I asked you for the privacy of our room for a while."

"You were a good few hours in there."

"Yep. He had a lot to tell me. He told me about his childhood and his father and how he really met Luke. I'm guessing that's what Luke has just been talking to you about."

"Yes, but I'm still confused. It's like he is still hiding something, like he is only saying part of the story. I don't think he really knew how to tell me, either. He was almost stuttering through it."

"Well Harley told me the whole truth, and obviously that is what Luke also knows. But Harley doesn't want people to know about his past. What I can tell you is that he had a bad start to life because of his dad. So, he and Luke just say they are brothers, and as their parents are married, people just assume that is it. What did Luke tell you? I'll try to help."

"That they were thrown together, and he was forced to accept Harley for a short while as his dad fostered him for about six months. He said that after about a week, he had to take Harley to his school, but they hadn't really got on at first. He told me that the story about the bully was true, and that was what helped to build their friendship. He said that they became closer and closer, and now they are best mates."

"Yeah, I was told that too. It's lovely. Luke's not hiding anything there, only the why Harley was fostered. His dad was mean. His mum and Harley went into hiding, but for a little while, his mum needed some help which is why Harley was put with a foster family. Once Harley returned to his mum, Luke and Harley were already best mates. So that's how Harley's mum met Luke's dad. They continued to let their boys be friends, and then you know the rest."

"Oh, that makes more sense and will be why Luke seemed cagey on parts."

Lizzie and Meg continued chatting for a while and then went to get some drinks. They decided that after everything they were allowed to relax back with some cocktails. By the time Harley and Luke arrived, Lizzie had just reached the last chapter of her book. Meg, who was a faster reader, had just finished it. Luke seemed nervous and wandered over tentatively. Meg saw him relax on his lounger. She went straight up to him, placed her knees on either side of him on the lounger, lay against his chest and gave him such a big kiss. Lizzie just smiled. Harley went to Lizzie, gave her a kiss and asked what that was all about.

"I don't think Luke really knew what to say when it came to the discussion earlier. Meg told me he was cagey about you. I've told her you had a bad childhood because of your father, that your mum needed some help looking after you for a while and that Luke's dad fostered you for that short time. At that point she understood why his story still seemed like it was missing a lot of truth."

"Did you tell her any details?"

Lizzie shook her head. "I promised I wouldn't, but I did tell her that you had told me everything, including the details that you didn't want me to share with anyone."

Harley took a deep breath and sighed. "Thank you. You're very kind and special. When we get home, I want you to meet my mum."

"Oh wow. I knew we were serious with the 'I love you' and the truth-telling." Lizzie suddenly becomes very nervous. "But what if she doesn't like me?"

"She will love you. I know she will."

"You seem very confident about that."

"Of course I am. You're gorgeous, you're kind, you're understanding and you treat me like a person." Between every few words Harley had kissed her.

"Like a person? What?" Lizzie laughed, all confused by that statement. "Of course I treat you like a person. What does that mean?"

"One thing about me is that I'm usually seen as an object because of my looks. That's why I've never had a girlfriend. Until now." Harley smiled at Lizzie, and she smiled back.

Meg was still sat straddling Luke. As she broke away from the kiss she had just surprised him with, he asked her if they could go on another date night tonight. They got up and she came over to get her shoes. "You two best entertain yourselves tonight. Luke wants to take me out, just the two of us."

"Have fun," Lizzie replied. She turned to Harley. "Right," she said. "What are we doing for our second date night?"

"Shall we go and book a meal?"

Harley and Lizzie went to book a table and then returned

to the pool. Ever since he mentioned girls seeing him as an object, she couldn't help but look round. She hadn't noticed before, but she kept seeing girls looking over at Harley. The more attention she paid to it, the more she realised that most girls were not just staring at him. They also seemed to be talking about him.

Lizzie was getting a little anxious about the girls staring. She trusted him. After all, he had never paid anyone else any attention and he said he had never even been inclined to go out with any of them when he was single. But she couldn't help it.

"I'm going to take a swim. You want to join me?"

"No, I'm going to sit and finish my chapter. When Meg and I finish our books, we chat about them, so I'd like to get it finished." Plus, she wanted to observe from a distance for a bit, hoping to put her mind at ease.

Lizzie sat down on her sun lounger. Picking up her book, she heard two girls nearby talking. She listened in. She knew she was being nosey, and it wasn't like her, but with all the stares and whispers she had seen, she wanted to see if her suspicions were right. The girls were on loungers to the side of Lizzie, so she could hear them clearly. However, Harley and Lizzie had been standing behind the girls when Harley gave her a kiss before walking to the pool.

"What the … Oh wow, dreamy," one of the girls said as her gaze followed Harley all the way to the pool.

"Oh my. Look at those muscles, that arse," said the second.

"Umm, to have that naked, in my bed, would be fantastic."

"Hey, he might prefer me."

"I saw him first, though, so I definitely get first dibs."

"Or we could share!" The second girl laughed.

Just then their mouths dropped. Lizzie followed their gazes and noticed Harley was getting out of the pool. His dripping wet muscles glistened in the sun. Even Lizzie had to take a sharp breath and she bit her lower lip. As he walked up to his lounger, he had to walk straight past the bottom of the girls' loungers. They must have thought he was walking towards them as they smiled. The first girl shouted out, "Hello, sexy. Coming to look for some pleasure?"

Harley continued walking. He didn't even glance at them.

"How about you take a seat next to me? Let me rub some sun cream into your sexy body."

Harley still just kept walking. They watched him walk straight past them. Their faces dropped with a disgusted expression as he leant over and gave Lizzie a kiss.

"Did you not hear that?" Lizzie asked.

"What?" he asked, completely oblivious to why she had asked.

"Those girls."

"Oh, not really, I don't take much notice of what girls like that say anymore."

"So, this is what you meant earlier, when you said they treat you like an object?"

"Yes." He looked at Lizzie strangely. "Had you not noticed this until I said something?"

"No. I think I was too busy looking at you and objectifying you," Lizzie said with a worried expression on her face.

"You don't objectify me, not like that. Anyway, I don't

mind you staring and thinking about what you'll do to me later. The difference was that you spoke to me, you listened to me, and now you know me inside and out." He always smiled when he got to make something sound dirty. Lizzie just leant forward and kissed him.

Harley and Lizzie split off to get changed for date night. When she got to the room, Meg was there getting ready too. "Hi. So, what happened to make Luke ask you for another date tonight?"

"I'm not really sure. I gave him a kiss after you told me why he might have been so cagey, and he just suddenly asked me. He hadn't said anything about it."

"You didn't ask him?"

"I don't like to. Might ask him tonight though."

"So what room are you sleeping in tonight?" Lizzie asked, "Not that you'll be doing much sleeping!"

"We haven't actually said anything about after, but he is coming here once he's ready."

"Meg, have you noticed how many girls stare at Harley?"

Meg looked at her strangely, questioningly. "Yes, why?"

"Harley said something earlier to me about me meeting his mother. I got a bit nervous and said what if she doesn't like me, to which he replied that she would because amongst other things, I don't objectify him. I'd never seen it before, but after that I noticed how many girls talk about him and stare at him, let alone shout out to him."

"Yeah, I've noticed it quite a lot. Luke said he struggled with the attention at first, but then when he realised they were all just being shallow and wanted him just for his looks and popularity, he decided enough was enough and things changed. Luke was telling me that Harley never even properly spoke to a girl after that, never let one get this close anyway. He never really cared what people thought of him, but he stopped caring completely, ignoring everything like that. And he started to choose his friends more carefully."

"I can't believe I've been so blinded by his looks myself that I hadn't noticed this."

"You've not. Well, I suppose you have been in new relationship world, where things are all happy and no one else is around."

"True. Thanks, that makes me feel better."

"Meeting his mum sounds good."

Lizzie and Meg continued to get ready for their second date night. They couldn't believe they were going to have a second romantic dinner. They felt truly spoilt.

Chapter 11

Second Date

About an hour later, the expected knock arrived. Harley and Luke usually only gave them just enough time to get ready. They both stood there, ready for date night and they looked great. Luke was wearing light blue shorts and a white and blue patterned shirt. Harley wore his typical black shorts. This time he was wearing a black shirt with a gold pattern which spread like flames from his left shoulder down the front and back. There was plenty of time before the reservations, so they had brought cocktails for the girls and lagers for them. Harley wrapped his arms around her and leaned in to give her a kiss. Lizzie whispered to Harley, asking him to discuss which rooms for later before leaving them to it while she went to finish getting ready. She had answered the door in a towel; she had just finished putting her makeup on. She zipped up her dress, one of her favourites, a black and white, figure-hugging short dress.

When she next appeared, Harley's jaw dropped. Laughing, Luke reached over and made a point of shutting it. Meg came out a few moments later, leaving Luke's mouth gaping. Harley returned the favour, shutting Luke's mouth, and laughed, a lot. They both commented on how wonderful the girls looked.

"You saw us in nice dresses yesterday," Meg said.

They both answered at the same time, basically saying, "Yeah, but you look even more gorgeous tonight." Everyone laughed.

"So, what time is your meal?" Lizzie asked Meg.

"Seven."

"And what room are you two staying in?" Lizzie asked.

"Umm," Luke stuttered, looking rather shy.

"You two not discussed that yet? Harley, I left you to find out!" she said cheekily with a smile. "OK. Well Meg, are you all right in the guys' room tonight?"

"Yep."

"OK, sorted. Luke and Meg in the guys' room. Harley and I in here. Men, they can't do anything," she joked with a smiled.

Harley leant in towards Lizzie and whispered in her ear, "You'll pay for that comment later."

"Is that a promise?"

"Definitely," he replied biting his lip followed by his little sexy smile. His eyes, sparkling and full of desire, were fixed on hers.

Luke and Meg went off for their meal shortly after the drinks were finished, but Harley and Lizzie still had half an hour. Harley turned to her and kissed her passionately. "I love hanging out with Luke and Meg, but sometimes I just need to be alone with you," Harley told Lizzie.

Lizzie smiled back. "I feel the same sometimes."

They shared more kisses before they realised that they had been kissing and caressing each other too long and were going to be late for their meal. "Oh dear, we best go," Lizzie said.

"You might want to run a brush through your hair first. I think I got a little carried away."

Lizzie looked in the mirror. Some of her hair was ruffled from where Harley had run his fingers through it. She freshened up and they briskly walked to the restaurant.

When they arrived they were escorted to their table. Harley ordered a bottle of sparkling wine. As they sat down, Harley reached out his hand. Lizzie reciprocated by placing her hand in his and he held it tight.

"Are you OK after today?" she asked.

"Yeah. It was nice to be able to open up to you. With what happened this morning, I was very worried about how we would move forward, but the fact you knew something was wrong made me feel comfortable enough to open up to you. Because of what happened that memory just seemed to flood back and it consumed my thoughts. Until I opened up to you I had no idea that it was still weighed on me."

"I'm glad you did. Childhood memories affect us all in different ways. You had probably been subconsciously suppressing it."

"Yes, I feel a lot freer now. Are you still happy to carry on this relationship after the holiday?"

"Of course. Why wouldn't I?" she asked.

"I suppose I'm still nervous. We are meant to be in the fun getting-to-know-you stage of our new relationship, not confessing all our deep, dark secrets. I also worry about how much I told you about my childhood."

"You worry too much. It made me feel sad, especially when I think about what you and your mum had to endure.

But that's it. Something outside your control or something in your past is not going to scare me off."

"I suppose I'm just nervous that you might not have wanted a future with me because of that."

Lizzie smiled. She didn't really know what to say to that. She was stuck repeating the phrase, "A future with me". All she could think was, *Did he really mean it the way it sounded?* but she didn't dare ask.

They enjoyed their meal, but they really enjoyed getting to know each other's pasts more. He asked her questions about her childhood, her parents, and her brother. He asked about her and Meg's friendship. Lizzie asked about his mum and Luke's dad, how they all got on with them being two families that had come together. Three courses and a whole bottle of sparkling wine later, they wandered down to the bar for more drinks.

They decided to walk the long way round and get some fresh air as their food was settling. As they left the restaurant, Harley took Lizzie's hand, interlocking their fingers. They walked around the stream, past the spa, and along the outskirts of the complex, where they could see the moon glistening on the calm sea.

Entering the bar, Harley went to get the drinks, while Lizzie chose a table. Lizzie sat waiting, facing the bar. She could see Harley was ordering the drinks. But then she suddenly saw something that made her feel very anxious. A young girl was approaching Harley. At that point Harley stood upright, looked over at Lizzie and smiled at her. Just as he was, the girl brushed past his arm. Harley's automatic response was to move his arm away. She moved to stand in front of him, being very flirtatious and attentive to him.

Lizzie could see Harley's expression. He appeared annoyed and irritated by her interruption. All Lizzie could see of her was the back of her skimpy, bright, silvery outfit. She ran her fingers down his upper arm and he moved away very quickly. The drinks he had been waiting for arrived—thankfully very quickly. Harley looked at the barman with a grateful expression thanking him for being quick. The barman laughed. He had seen this type of thing plenty of times before.

As Harley walked over to Lizzie, the girl kept trying to stay in front of him, trying to block his way. She was swaying all over the place, staggering backwards and forwards, and still trying to get him to come back to her table and meet her girlfriends. But Harley was having none of it. Lizzie could hear him saying things like, "Sorry, I have a girlfriend" and "Please, I'm going back to my girlfriend now." He got back to the table. And because she had followed him, he made a big gesture, giving Lizzie a kiss. She finally got the message.

"Girlfriend? Was that just to get her to leave you alone?" Lizzie asked. He had only referred to her as his girlfriend once so far and that was to Lizzie.

"No, you are my girlfriend, aren't you?"

"Just hadn't really thought of calling myself that and calling you my boyfriend."

"Don't people usually acknowledge they are girlfriend and boyfriend before they admit they are in love?" he questioned.

"True."

"And if I'm taking you to meet my mum after this holiday, what else would I introduce you as?"

Lizzie smiled and gave him a peck on his lips. "I am so lucky to have found someone as wonderful as you."

"I think it's me who should be saying that to you."

They stayed at the bar for a couple of drinks and Lizzie dragged Harley up to the dance floor for a couple of songs. They then took a drink back to the room and stayed up most of the night talking and cuddling. He didn't get her back for the comment she made earlier like he had promised, but it was a wonderful night. They enjoyed just being together.

Chapter 12

The One Week Anniversary

The next day, after breakfast, Lizzie and Meg joined up to play tennis while the guys joined some organised sports on the beach. Meg told Lizzie all about her date night. Meg was so happy about how well she was getting on with Luke and how much they had in common. She told Lizzie that she was still nervous about what would happen after the holiday, especially when they spilt off for their different universities. But she was trying her best to focus on the now. Lizzie told Meg about the girl trying to get Harley to go back to her table and they had a good laugh about it.

They talked most of the morning and discussed the books they recently finished. In the afternoon they relaxed by the pool and enjoyed a couple of mocktails and did plenty of reading. By the time Harley and Luke came back from the beach, they were halfway through their books. Harley sat and gave Lizzie a kiss. "How is my gorgeous girlfriend?"

"I still can't get used to that." She leaned in, giving him a cuddle. "Oh gosh, you're covered."

"Sorry. Been playing volleyball and landed in the sand a few times."

"It looks like it was more than a few."

"Maybe" he joked with his soft, sexy smirk.

Luke was getting all comfortable next to Meg on her sun lounger. It was great to see them so comfortable together. He was so stand-offish at the beginning of the holiday, and now they seemed so happy with each other. It made Lizzie beam with happiness for them. She hadn't seen Meg this connected with anyone else. Lizzie caught Harley looking over and smiling. He looked happy for them too.

Harley and Luke had a court booked for tennis but seeing how Luke had become so cosy with Meg, he asked Lizzie to join him instead as he didn't want to disturb them. They walked straight over to the tennis courts and found their court. Harley was much better at tennis than Lizzie and that was with him going easy on her. Afterwards, they took the long trail back to the swimming pool, stopping to play pool on the way.

That night they all decided to have a night off from each other. Lizzie and Meg went for dinner together, followed by drinks and few games of pool. They had just been thinking about one more round before they headed back to their room when Harley and Luke entered the bar. The guys waved and went straight to the bar. They stayed round the bar for a while, but Meg went fetch some more drinks and told them they were welcome to join. They had only just been for dinner and decided to have a couple of drinks before heading back to their room. They all sat around the table, laughing and joking. A couple of drinks later, Harley and Luke escorted the girls back to their room. Harley put his arm around Lizzie and whispered, "I so want to ask you to stay with me, but I think we both need to catch up on some sleep."

"I think you read my mind," Lizzie joked. He gave her a long, lingering kiss and wished her a good night sleep.

Harley placed his elbow on Luke's shoulder. "Parting is such sweet sorrow, that we shall say good night till it be morrow," Harley announced.

"Good night, fair maidens," Harley and Luke said together as they bowed, giving the girls a kiss on the backs of their hands. Lizzie and Meg went into their room giggling and giddy.

Harley put his arm over Luke's shoulders. "Just you and me, my mate. Oh, but how I'm going to miss having her to hold," Harley said dreamily.

"Well, you're not holding me all night, Hars."

"Oh please," he said, expressing a jokingly sad and pouting face.

The next day, Lizzie and Meg lazed around the pool, enjoying their books and generally enjoying being on holiday. Harley and Luke played more group sports, tennis, some games of pool and bumped into the girls when they went for a swim in the afternoon. They all met up and enjoyed dinner together before splitting off for more sleep in their own beds.

The following day for Lizzie and Meg was the same. They hung out around the pool again. Harley and Luke joined them each mealtime and came for a swim with them a few times in between the organised sports they joined in with. On Friday, Harley and Luke announced that it was date night.

"It's been a week since we met you on the plane. We need to celebrate that," Harley said.

"Where have you booked?" asked Meg.

"Pez 43," Luke replied.

Lizzie and Meg looked at each other in wonder. They had walked past that restaurant so many times and had really wanted to see what it was like.

That evening back in their room, Lizzie and Meg were getting ready. "I'm glad I brought this dress with me now. And I'm so glad I didn't wear it for the other date nights," Meg said to Lizzie.

"I know what you mean. This restaurant is amazing. But did you realise it's not included in our package?"

"Oh really. No. I had assumed, but I never actually looked at it properly. I didn't think we would end up in there."

There was the knock at the door. The guys stood there all dreamy looking, each with a flower in hand. Harley put it in Lizzie's hair, while Luke placed Meg's within the shoulder straps of her dress. They held out their elbows to Meg and Lizzie, who linked their arms with them. The guys escorted Lizzie and Meg to the restaurant, arm in arm.

At the restaurant, the couples split off, heading to their tables. As they sat, they were each presented with a bottle of champagne, which the guys had pre-ordered. This also wasn't included in the all-inclusive price. The girls really were being spoilt.

It was an amazing three-course, candlelit meal with amazing company. Each course was small in portion but rich and delicious. They felt full after. After the meal, Harley took Lizzie on a romantic stroll down the beach, stopping right where they shared their first kiss. His form towered over, making her feel as weak as she did when they first met. He stroked the side of her cheek and tilted her chin up a little before he locked their lips in a fervent and intoxicating, long, open-mouthed kiss. His tongue danced round her mouth slowly and tenderly. Harley felt her weaken slightly and picked her up. She wrapped her arms and legs round him tight, and the kiss became deeper and extremely luscious. Eventually, though, he pulled away.

"We need to go back to the room," he said rather breathlessly.

She loosened her grip and he lowered her down.

Harley escorted her straight back to his room. The guys must have already organised this between themselves. Back in the room there was another bottle of Champagne. Harley was really going all out this night.

"Harley, this is amazing, but I can't let you pay for all of it. Please, let me pay half."

"Nope. This is my treat. I realise it's only been a week but it's been a long week. I've fallen madly in love with you. You are the most wonderful person I know. I have never told anyone my story, but I trust you and" he paused, taking a slow breath, "I just can't believe I've been this lucky to find you."

Lizzie could only smile. She was shocked. He was always shocking her with the amazing things he said. She managed to take a deep breath. "I love you too."

"We will do similar celebration for our one-month anniversary, back in England," he said.

"Really?" she said, again shocked.

"Would you stop being so shocked. I want to be with

you, not just for this holiday and not just until we go to university. I want to be with you forever."

Oh wow. *He really meant that comment about the future.*

Lizzie sat on the sofa while he opened the Champagne and poured them each a glass. He sat next to her and took her hands in his. "Lizzie," he said very seriously, "I need you to know so you can stop being so shocked all the time."

"I can't promise not to be, but I'll try."

"Well, that's good enough. Right." Harley took a deep breath and swallowed before continuing. He seemed nervous. "Lizzie, I love you. I want to be with you. I want you to meet my parents, my bandmates, and my other mates. I want you to be part of my life. Forever. And one day, when the time is right, I intend on marrying you."

Lizzie was silent. A shocked look swept across her face. "Youuu … want toooo … umm." She took a big gulp. Lizzie was visibly shaking now.

"Marry you? Yes. At the right point in our lives together, yes, I want us to be married. I want you, forever."

"Wow."

"To wow," Harley joked, clinking his glass with hers.

They had a drink and Lizzie regained her thoughts. "What happens if I don't want marriage?" she asked, trying to control a smile.

It was Harley who looked shocked now. He didn't know what to say. His face suddenly dropped in sadness and tears actually formed in his eyes, which he tried to hide as he put his drink down.

"Oh, Harley, I'm sorry. I was just trying to lighten the mood with it being so serious. I don't mean it."

Harley tried his best to smile, but without success.

"Harley," she moved his chin so she could look in his eyes. She straddled him, getting as close as possible. As calmly and clearly as she could, she told him, "I love you, and I want everything you have described. I only want them with you. No one else will do." She clasped her lips on his. "I'm sorry for my bad-timed joke. I really do want everything you have just described. That's one reason why I'm always so shocked when you say it as it feels like you're reading my mind."

He smiled, and it turned into a proper cheeky grin. "I know. I was just getting you back for that horrid question." He tickled her waist. Her body ended up twisting and turning as she tried to stop him from tickling her. They ended up laughing about it.

They continued to sit together, chatting away. Harley poured a second glass which he placed on the bedside table. He came back into the lounge, and taking her hand, he escorted her to his bed. He slid his hands up her arms and across her shoulders. Sliding one hand down her back, he took the zip with his fingers and caused her strapless dress to fall to the floor. With the other, he let his fingers glide through her hair. He affectionately kissed her while holding her extremely close. A wave of pleasure and pure ecstasy surged through their bodies, and Lizzie started to feel all weak again. She unbuttoned his shirt, letting her fingers float over his well-defined muscles up to his shoulders before pushing his shirt down his arms, letting it fall to the floor. His trousers were off by the time she finished stroking her fingertips over his muscles. He embraced her close again, leant her over, and they fell on the bed. His hands stroked down to her knees, which he pulled up as he knelt over her.

Then putting some of his weight on her, he came close, and they kissed. It was deep, affectionate and sensuous.

This luxurious and pleasurable teasing went on for the whole glass of Champagne. Occasionally he kissed her skin with the Champagne still in his mouth. His lips felt like they were popping against her skin as the Champagne bubbles popped. Some of the Champagne even drizzled from his lips down her body and the bubbles, against her skin, made her quiver. Her hunger for him intensified especially when he kissed her inner thighs and between her legs. When he did this, he allowed the bubbling Champagne to escape from his lips and her pleasure erupted as a satisfied moan.

About an hour later, he poured the remaining Champagne into their glasses, and they both took a bathroom break. As she sauntered back in, she noticed he had placed all the clothes neatly on Luke's bed. He was sitting on the bed with the glasses in his hands. She walked up close and placed her knees on either side of him. As she started to lower herself onto him, he kissed her stomach and released the Champagne he had in his mouth. It trickled down her stomach, making her tremble as it went over her most sensitive area. There wasn't much in each glass, so they paused their teasing and had the few mouthfuls each that were left.

They had learnt so much about each other's bodies. They knew what each other liked, and tonight they used this to their advantage. The teasing was slow and intimate. Lizzie pushed him down onto the bed and began to tease him, trying to make him feel all the sensations that he had just caused to surge within her. She began by trailing open-mouthed kisses all over his chest, concentrating on each nipple. She had pushed his hands under his back so he couldn't keep teasing her. She continued to travel her lips down his abdomen, his breathy moans getting louder, and the sensations pulsing through him faster as she came closer to his hips. Her lips brushed over his member. Then she let her tongue stroke it from the base to the tip, where she kissed him. In one quick movement he freed his hands, grabbed her tightly, pulled her up to him, and then flipped them over.

Now he was on top, and the teasing was over. Lizzie could see his heightened desire burning in his eyes. He pressed some of his body weight against her. Then stopped. They maintained eye contact as they regained some of their control. He slowly lowered his lips and placed a loving kiss against hers. Their bodies started gradually and slowly to move in sync, waves of passion building.

"Harley, have you remembered?"

He placed the packet to her lips and she realised he must have just been reaching for it. After placing the protection on, he lined up their hips. She brought her knees right up as they glided together. Their movements started slowly. Their hips rocked together, their bodies firmly pressing and gliding over each other. Lizzie needed more, and Harley's breathing told her that he was trying to keep control, trying to make everything last. Lizzie squeezed him tighter; a breathy moan escaped him. She slid her nails down his back, and his muscles clenched, forcing his body deeper into her. Her nails were just starting to float down his back, starting at his shoulder, when a strong climax overtook her body. Her body pulsated and contracted, causing her to tighten her grip on him. Her nails that were floating down his back dug in and scraped down his back instead. The intense and sudden pain sent pleasure pulsating throughout his body, and he was hit by his own intense climax.

By the end, their hearts were pounding, and they were exhausted from the passion they had just shared. "I think you got me good just then," said Harley.

He was still lying on his front, so she moved slightly so she could look over his shoulder. She had a pang of guilt as she saw she had left two scratch marks down his back. "Oh gosh, I'm sorry. I've really scratched you badly down your back."

"That's OK. It felt incredible." He pulled her back down and wrapped himself around her, giving her a kiss. "I really enjoyed *all* of that." he said flirtatiously.

"Me too. It was amazing."

When Lizzie awoke the next morning, they were still all cuddled up, and she still felt all the passion that she had last night.

Start of the Second Week

Lizzie and Harley really enjoyed spending time together. They continued to talk about everything. They had learnt so much about each other in the last week and felt incredibly comfortable with each other. She thought he seemed dependable and sensitive, and he was always understanding and accepting of anything she told him. When they first met, he was so confident and assertive, but he seemed to have a barrier Lizzie didn't think was likely to be broken. She still saw all of this but only as his outward appearance to others. Like Luke, Lizzie had been let through that protective barrier on a deep level. Meg had been accepted also, and they all seemed very good friends. Knowing his history, Lizzie could understand how and why he had developed this protective external, almost bad boy persona, but she felt lucky to know the real him. He always made her feel very special. It was not just the attention to detail, it was the way he hugged her, his tender touch, the way he always told her the truth, and how he always told her how he felt.

Harley was vulnerable around Lizzie. From the moment she had bumped into him in the airport, something seemed different about her. Harley was thankful when they ended up at the same resort, and when she seemed to be interested in him, he knew he needed her in his life. The vulnerability made him scared, but he also knew that she had accepted him. And even more important, she had accepted his past. He had never shared that with anyone outside the family before, and now that made her more valuable to him.

Lizzie still worried about what would happen after the holiday. They had been able to spend as much time together as they wanted, talk about everything, and do what they wanted. They spent most nights curled up together. The time they had spent apart she couldn't help but think about him, and she even missed him. If this was how she felt now, what was going to happen when they landed and had to go their separate ways? What were her parents going to think? His outward appearance appealed to Lizzie. You could tell he was a fan of rock and heavy metal music from his hair and clothes, but she knew her parents would not accept him as her boyfriend, at least not easily. Would they just think it was a short-term thing and not try to get to know him? It was all jumbling up in her head, and although she was only just halfway through the holiday, she was starting to become anxious about it.

Harley tilted her chin up, lifting her gaze to meet his. He gave her a kiss and a nice tight squeeze. "Is everything OK?" he asked.

"Yeah. I'm curled up in your arms. Everything is great," she said, smiling.

"What's really going on in that mind of yours?"

"What do you mean?" she asked.

"I'm not sure. You just seem deep in thought."

"Oh, I have been thinking about what my parents might think of you, and I started to worry a little."

"Oh, I guess they will find me unsuitable then?"

She started telling him all the thoughts that had been going round in her mind, and he laughed sweetly. "Don't worry about that for now. I promise to be correct and polite," he assured her, smiling.

"I know. Just ignore me. I shouldn't be worrying about it now anyway. We have another week of holiday left."

Harley and Luke were booked on the same flight as Lizzie and Meg on the way home. The girls had discussed swapping seats, so they could cuddle up with their men. They had joked about joining the Mile High Club, but when they had actually started to discuss it seriously, it was not something they wanted to do. They joked that toilet was far too small to make it pleasurable.

Harley and Lizzie spent the day together, just the two of them. They played tennis, went for a walk on the beach, and swam in the sea. They had been for a long walk around the resort and found an airgun shooting range. They stopped by and had a try. Lizzie managed to get a better score than Harley, but she was not sure if he had let her win, or if he just wasn't any good.

As they walked through the reception area, there was a sign about an excursion. The picture made it look interesting, so they asked the Rep about it. It was a full day boat trip, leaving Monday. It would give them chance to see bottlenose dolphins and the coasts of Spain and Morocco. It also would be stopping in Gibraltar and they would have a chance to wander through the main streets. Harley and Lizzie decided to go together, but it was also something Lizzie knew Meg would like, so they decided to book it after they spoke to Meg and Luke.

Having bumped into them a few times, Harley and Lizzie knew exactly where to find them, the pool. Within half an hour, the four of them were at the Rep's desk booking the excursion. Luke, Lizzie and Meg were completing their forms, but Harley had been talking to the Rep. Handing in their forms, Lizzie and Meg discovered that Harley and Luke had already paid for them. "Thank you. You didn't have to," Lizzie said to Harley.

"I know. But I don't do things for you because I have to. It's because I want to."

For the rest of the day the four hung out round the pool, drinking, reading and generally having fun together. Then Luke saw the claw marks down Harley's back. "Who attacked you?" he joked.

"Oh, we got a little carried away."

"Bet that hurt!"

All Harley could do was give Luke a big smile and his eyebrows rose briefly, which told that it had been pleasurable. Harley and Luke continued to make jokes about it for a while as they were getting ready to jump into the water. Meg had overheard the conversation and as Harley turned to jump into the pool, she gasped at the marks and her eyes went wide. "Lizzie, that was you?"

"Yeah," she cringed. "I didn't mean to scratch him, but …" She just smiled and shrugged her shoulders. She didn't know what else to say.

That evening they split off, Lizzie and Meg went to dinner followed by the bar. But they didn't see Harley and Luke this time. They were a little disappointed that they hadn't bumped into them, but it was certainly a good night for the two girls. They headed back to their room about eleven o'clock with a couple a drinks and stayed up chatting. They were rather tipsy by time they finished the drinks and they heard a little tap on the door. They looked at each other. Lizzie walked over and looked through the peephole. "It's Luke and Harley."

She opened the door. They were leaning on each other as if they needed the support to stand. They had been in the restaurant for a while just drinking until they were told to leave. Then they went to the bar. They were a little drunk and very funny with it. They said that they wanted to come over for a goodnight kiss. Lizzie and Meg decided to escort them back to their room. Each guy wrapped his arms around his girl. It was probably more so that they had something to lean on and keep them stable.

"Luke, where is your key?" asked Meg as they arrived at the room door.

"My front pocket," Luke slurred.

Meg slid her hand into his front pocket, trying to find the key.

"Oh Meg, that does feel good."

Lizzie burst out laughing. It was the first time she had heard him say something even slightly frisky.

Lizzie and Meg helped the guys to their beds. They collapsed on them, bringing the girls down with them both. Luke had dragged Meg down and now kissed her, his hands running over her back. Lizzie landed on Harley's lap and he gave her a loving big cuddle and kiss. "You're lovely," he slurred.

"You're drunk," she stated with a giggle.

"And? That's OK, isn't it?" He looked at her with puppy dog eyes, his sweet smile spreading across his face.

"Harley, you're so sweet. I love you." He smiled and gave her another big kiss.

Harley and Luke started to fall asleep, so the girls made sure they were comfy before they went back to their room. The guys had been a little drunk, but they weren't bad. They weren't so intoxicated that the girls had to worry about them being sick in their sleep. They had told Lizzie and Meg that they had knocked on their door gently so that they didn't wake them if they had been asleep, but the girls were both glad they hadn't missed them.

Lizzie and Meg spent Sunday morning lounging round the pool. There wasn't any organised activities and everything was quiet. Harley and Luke, only just emerging from their room, came to find them for an early lunch, and they all went together. Late afternoon Lizzie and Meg went back to their room to freshen up for dinner. They had wanted to pack ready for the excursion. As usual, Luke and Harley brought some drinks over to their room, which they enjoyed before walking over to the restaurant. After dinner they stopped for a couple of drinks in the bar. Lizzie and Meg started to take the micky out of them for last night's late-night call. They had remembered coming over to the girls' room and knocking. They even remembered them answering the door, but they didn't remember how they got back to their room. The next fun-filled hour was spent telling them all about it. Looking back, it was all rather funny. Harley had been leaning on Lizzie for support, and as he was much taller than her, she had struggled to keep him upright. He kept stopping, apologising for being drunk and telling her how much he loved her.

"I think you stopped me about ten times in that short walk," Lizzie joked.

Lizzie and Meg were in hysterics. Harley and Luke were also seeing the funny side of it, but when it came to Lizzie and Meg describing how Meg was trying to hold up a drunk Luke, they all burst into laughter. Lizzie and Meg acted it out. Meg was supporting Luke, played by Lizzie, who was trying to put all her weight on Meg. Harley was falling about laughing at that point as he could picture Meg, who in comparison to muscular Luke, was quite petite. Playing Luke, Lizzie was putting her hand on Meg's cheek and slurring, "I'm sorry," and "You're lovely." They stopped the banter as they realised that Luke was embarrassed by his actions.

Meg went to sit with him. "I liked looking after you last night, and I managed fine. It wasn't as bad as we are making out."

He still didn't seem to accept that all was fine and that this was all just a joke, so Lizzie changed the subject to tomorrow's trip, saying how much she was looking forward to it.

Meg leant over and whispered to Luke, "Luke, by the way …" Then she became too quiet for Lizzie and Harley to hear.

Lizzie knew exactly what she had said, though, as his expression altered. His face suddenly dropped. He developed a wide-eyed, worried and scared expression.

"What? I said that to you last night?" He almost shouted it. His voice filled with the panic his face displayed.

"Yes," Meg whispered.

Meg had told Lizzie what he had said and although she wanted to sit and watch this unfold, she also knew they needed some privacy. Lizzie took Harley's hand and led him into a dance.

"Why did we move? We've still got full drinks," Harley asked.

"Last night Luke told Meg that he really likes her and thinks he is falling in love with her. Meg told me on the way back from your room, after you both fell asleep. She is really happy. I think she feels the same way. From his reaction, I'm guessing she just told him what he said. That's why I brought you over here, to give them some privacy to talk about it."

"Oh wow. We really must have had a lot to drink to bring his reservations down that far. He is always so guarded with his feelings, even when he has had lots to drink. I'm sorry about last night, especially the fact that you had to take care of us. It must have been great to see us slumped there fast asleep," he said as he ran his hand down her back and pulled her in closer.

"It's OK. It was nice to see you. And it was also nice to be able to take care of you. Plus, you apologised so much last night, you're already forgiven. You were very sweet looking when you were drifting to sleep, but as we were leaving, you both were starting to snore. Loudly." A smile appeared.

"Really? I don't snore, do I?" Harley asked with a worried look.

Lizzie laughed. "No, only messing with you."

"Phew. Oh, I spoke to my mum yesterday. I told her all about you."

Lizzie gasped. Her expression showed panic as she

processed what he said. "What? You've told her about me already?"

"Yeah. She can't wait to meet you. In fact, I, umm", he paused.

"Why are you going all quiet and shy now? That's not like you."

He took a deep breath. "I would like to take you out on the Saturday, after we get back home." He paused. "I'm not sure what yet, and I didn't know if you were working or had plans, but well …" He paused again. "I was thinking I could at least take you out for a meal and maybe, maybe you could come over to mine afterwards, meet my parents, and I've, umm talked to her about you staying over in my room, if that's OK with you."

"I've not got any plans that day, apart from unpacking and washing. What time are you free from?"

"All day. I will come over to yours, pick you up and we can go out for the day."

"That sounds good. I live close to a nature reserve. When you come over and we can go for a walk and have a picnic? If my parents are in, you can meet them before we go." Lizzie went a little nervous saying the last part. She had felt the anxiety build up. Her parents meeting Harley made her feel very anxious.

"Sounds like a plan. After, we will go over to mine. Pack yourself something nice to wear that night. You can get changed at mine and we will go out for a meal that evening. Oh, and pack yourself one of your nice bikinis also."

Lizzie looked at him confused.

"It's a surprise. I am presuming you're free the Sunday morning. Do you need to be home at a certain time?"

"No, I'm free all Sunday."

Harley smiled at her. He had seemed so nervous saying all that, and now he was beaming.

Both Lizzie and Harley felt so excited that they had just made arrangements to see each other after the holiday. All Lizzie could think about was how they would land on Friday evening and on the Saturday, he was going to spend the whole day with her, meeting her parents, taking her out for a meal, and she would be sleeping all cuddled up with him in his bed. And she was going to meet his parents. Talk about jumping in at the deep end. Lizzie had expected it to be a good few weeks or even months before she met his parents and she had definitely hoped to delay her parents meeting him.

Harley and Luke escorted the girls back to their room. They gave them overly extended kisses goodnight and went back to their room. They were all meeting at eight o'clock the next morning ready for the excursion and Lizzie was very excited. However, she was also excited about telling Meg all about Harley arranging to meet up with her after the holiday. And she couldn't wait to hear what went on between her and Luke.

Meg was excited when Lizzie told her about the weekend that Harley organised after the holiday. Lizzie asked Meg about what happened with Luke. "He told me that he meant it. He said he had been feeling it for a few days but was apprehensive about telling me in case it changed anything. I guess with him being drunk his worries disappeared."

"What happened then?"

"I told him I feel the same," she said in a rather nervous tone.

"That's great. I'm really pleased for you," Lizzie said, her excitement showing through.

"I'm still worried though. Relationships take work, but I bet it's much harder for long distance."

"I'm glad Harley is not too far from me at uni, but I feel sorry for you and Luke. But you know Meg, you'll be fine. You both have the same passions, the same ways of thinking. You'll have loads to talk about, and you can support each other, not only emotionally, but you will be great at helping each other with your work too. And that will give you even more excuses to talk."

"Yes, I think you're right. I'm sure we will be fine. We have been good at communicating so far, and when we are apart, that's all we will have."

Chapter 14

The Excursion

Monday, the day of the excursion, Lizzie and Meg were really excited. They loved going out on boats, and Meg's favourite sea creature was the dolphin. The weather was beautiful. In the morning they saw a pod of dolphins that swam at the bow of the boat for a while. They were really clear to see. The boat docked in Gibraltar and everyone got off to have a look around for two hours.

As Lizzie and Meg were getting off the boat, Lizzie asked, "Have you noticed the two girls eyeing up Harley and Luke?"

"Yes. They keep peering over and smiling."

"The amount of time they've been staring at them makes me feel a little uncomfortable," said Lizzie.

"And me. But we have nothing to worry about. Plus, I'm not sure if the guys have even noticed."

So far, the four of them had been acting more like a group of friends rather than affectionate couples. Harley and Luke went to the girls' room first, so they had given them their good morning kisses there, and they had all walked up to the reception area together. However, Lizzie and Meg had gone to the reception desk as they needed some extra water in their room. When they got back to the guys, they were chatting to the staff on the excursion, so they had hung back. Lizzie and Meg had seen the two girls at the hotel reception, eyes fixed on Harley and Luke, just before they boarded the coach. As a group they had gone right to the back, Luke sat next to Meg, and Lizzie sat with Harley. The guys had sat on the aisle seats with their arms wrapped around Lizzie and Meg. Harley and Lizzie were busy looking out the window and talking about the things they saw.

Boarding the boat, Lizzie and Meg had gone to sit down, saving seats for the guys. Harley and Luke went over to the bar in the centre of the boat to get drinks before setting sail. Being one of the last on the boat, many seats were already taken, so the girls ended up sitting opposite the guys.

After Gibraltar, the boat stopped in a quiet bay where everyone could go swimming in the crystal clear water. They had all taken snorkels and masks so that they could have a good look under the water. They were getting ready to jump in, and the two girls eyeing Luke and Harley did something that made Lizzie and Meg laugh so much, that they ended up with tears streaming down their cheeks. They could see the girls slowly shuffling over. The girl standing next to Harley raised her foot to take off her shoe and toppled right into him. Harley grabbed her arm to help her and looked over to Lizzie and Meg, as they had just burst out laughing so loudly. She stood there saying thank you. She smiled and fluttered her eyelashes. As she placed her hand on his bicep, she bit her lower lip. "Ooh such big, strong muscles," she said.

Harley was not impressed and his facial expression showed his annoyance. Then he looked over at Lizzie and Meg, who could still be heard laughing loudly. He and Luke shared a displeased look and just carried on getting ready. The girl did not like being ignored, so she stroked his shoulder and down his back, at which point Harley pushed her hand off his back. Lizzie was starting to feel a little jealous and had stopped laughing. The girl was still flirting with Harley. Lizzie was ready to jump into the water, but she just stood there, arms crossed and a mean look on her face. The other girl had started to flirt with Luke. Luke and Harley hadn't really spoken to the girls, but the girls were drooling all over them. Harley and Luke quickly and silently finished getting ready.

Lizzie and Meg, both ready, had been waiting for the guys. The girls were still trying their best to flirt with the guys, touching their biceps and getting very, very close to them. The guys had been backing off, putting their arms out to push them away. But the girls were adamant and tried everything. Lizzie whispered to Meg and when the girls were in the right position, Lizzie and Meg ran up to their men and wrapped their arms around their waists, *accidentally* bumping into the girls, who ended up falling into the water with a loud splash.

It was like the whole boat erupted with laughter. The staff helped the girls out of the water. They had still been fully dressed. As they sat on the side, the staff ensuring they were all right, Lizzie and Meg came up from behind, ready to jump in. "We are *so* sorry we caused you to fall in the water, but you really should have left our boyfriends alone." The girls frowned at Lizzie and Meg, who just smiled back.

Lizzie and Meg jumped into the water, quickly followed by the guys. As Harley and Luke resurfaced, they noticed the girls, now ready for the water, about to jump in. The guys dived under the water and swam right up to Lizzie and Meg. Harley wrapped his arms around Lizzie, landing a kiss on her lips, and Luke did the same to Meg. The expressions on the girls' faces were priceless. They seemed so frustrated and angry that Harley and Luke had seemed to ignore them and chosen to be with other girls. They reminded Lizzie of the type of spoilt rich kid who always got her way and she realised they weren't going to back off easily.

They spent the rest of the time in the sea messing about as well as swimming around, looking at the fish and the seabed. It was wonderful; there was so much to see. The bell rang to say it was time to get out and everyone made their way back to the boat. It was lunchtime and everyone was starving. Lizzie and Meg got two spaces each and sat down while Harley and Luke went up to collect the food boxes. The girls were stood right behind them and were trying to start a conversation with them, although Harley and Luke completely ignored them. They seemed deep in conversation with each other. The girls did not want to back down though, and kept clinging to them, feeling their biceps and trying to get their attention. Eventually the guys received the boxes and drinks and came back to sit with Lizzie and Meg.

"What is going on? Won't they just accept that you're not interested?" Lizzie asked.

"This is what happens when girls fancy Harley," Luke remarked.

"Yeah, but they are after you too!" Harley commented.

"True, but only cuz I'm with you."

"So what do you do?" Lizzie asked Harley.

"I normally just ignore them and they finally leave me alone. These two are *really* pushing it though." He sounded angry at the last part. "They know we are with you two. We told them we have girlfriends, but they keep saying they don't mind a one-night stand. I hate it when girls go that far," Harley said.

"They do seem rather desperate. From what they were saying, I don't think they are going to leave us alone anytime soon," Luke added.

"That's OK. It just means you have to give us extra cuddles and kisses and never leave our sides" said Meg, a huge smile on her face.

Harley sat next to Lizzie and put his arm around her. "You OK with this?"

"It's strange to see *my* man being hit on so much, but I trust you."

"Good, because I'm not going anywhere. I love you."

"I love you too. But just make sure you never leave our sides."

"Promise."

After lunch the boat headed back to port, where the coach would be waiting to take everyone back to the complex. Harley and Luke didn't move from their girlfriends' sides. They did everything as couples. They enjoyed a couple more rounds of drinks and watched out for the dolphins again at the bow. At one point Lizzie caught the girls staring over. They looked rather annoyed that they hadn't been able to secure dates with Harley and Luke yet. The girls were very pretty and Lizzie still felt rather jealous, especially since they still kept looking over at them. All she could think of was how much prettier than her they were.

Harley could obviously tell she still felt strange. He stood up, took her hand and walked her to the stern of the boat, where it was quieter. "You're not OK with this, are you?"

"No," she said with a heavy sigh. "I've never actually had a boyfriend and you are so good-looking, everyone will wonder what you are doing with me. I'm nowhere near as pretty as they are."

His expression changed. He became wide-eyed, shocked by what she said. He was still holding her hand and they were leaning against the railings of the boat. He released her hand and tenderly slid his fingers over her cheek. He continued to run his fingers up and through her hair. His light, feathery touch brought a spark of electricity to her. "You are everything to me. You are gorgeous and what makes you even more gorgeous is who you are. They are absolutely *nothing* compared to you." His voice was soft and gentle, but firm.

"But they are so pretty."

"Yes, I admit they are pretty, on the outside. But they are nowhere near as gorgeous as you. Plus, you are extra special in the fact that you have a gorgeous personality to go along with your gorgeous exterior."

Lizzie gave him a little shy smile. "You always seem to know what to say to make me feel better."

"Just as you know me so well too."

They stood there for a while, looking out to the sea and land, his arms enveloping her to try to keep her warm. He realised she was still shivering, so he took off his shirt and held it out for her. "Put this on." Then he pulled her in to hold her tightly against his bare, warm chest.

"Docking in thirty minutes," was announced over the speakers. They separated so they could visit the toilet to prepare for the thirty-minute coach ride. Harley said he would meet her back with Meg and Luke. When Lizzie came out of the toilet, she noticed that Harley wasn't with Luke and Meg. She panicked and a sudden pang of jealousy took hold of her. She looked over to the other side of the boat, where the male toilets were and saw Harley with the girl who had been feeling him up earlier. Lizzie was so consumed with jealousy that she was frozen. That was probably a good thing as it made her watch what was happening. Harley kept trying to move away from the girl and she just kept going for him. Her hands were all over him. He backed off or tried to move around her to leave, but she and her friend were creating barriers. Eventually he had backed off so much that he was against the side of the boat. That was now creating an extra barrier.

He saw Lizzie standing there and didn't take his eyes off her. He had such a worried expression on his face. He was concerned as to what Lizzie might be thinking of him. Lizzie had regained some control and walked over, the girl noticed her and reached up to kiss Harley. She was taller than Lizzie and better able to reach to Harley's lips than Lizzie could. He backed off really quickly; Lizzie didn't think she had ever seen him move so fast. As he moved away, he pushed his hands out which caused her to back off. He went straight over to Lizzie and cuddled her. "I'm so sorry," he said.

"It's not your fault," Lizzie said. And although she

believed that, she also couldn't stop thinking about how much effort the girls had just made. "Come on," she said, and they walked over to Meg and Luke.

Harley sat next to Luke. He hung his head, hiding it with his hands. "This is the worst I've ever known it," Harley told Luke.

"What is?"

"That stupid thing saw Lizzie and deliberately tried to break us up by trying to kiss me. I was able to move away, but only just in time. Lizzie saw everything." Harley was angry and upset.

"Oh." Luke put his hand on Harley's shoulder. Harley seemed distraught by the situation.

During their conversation, Meg looked over to the guys and then at Lizzie. Lizzie just seemed shocked. "What's going on?" Meg asked.

"That girl. She just tried to kiss Harley."

"Oh gosh."

"He backed off really quickly, but she did almost have her lips on his."

"Oh."

"I don't know what to do. No matter what she did, Harley was always backing off and trying to move away. But I, … I just, … I hate what I just saw."

Just then Luke spoke up, loud enough for Meg to hear. "Meg?" Luke gestured for her to come over to them. Meg went over. With what had just happened, Luke didn't want to leave the seat next to Harley empty in case the girl dived in quickly. Meg sat down next to Harley, and they started talking.

Meanwhile Luke sat with Lizzie. "I'm sorry, Lizzie."

"What do you mean?"

"Harley told me what happened. I've never seen it go this far before. He can't believe what just happened himself. Are you OK?"

"I'm just trying to process it. It was a shock, but I'll be OK."

"Harley is really worried this is going to change things between you both."

"Oh gosh, no. It wasn't him going after someone. He did absolutely nothing to encourage it. In fact, he has spent the whole boat trip telling her to go away."

Harley got up and went over to the rail at the edge of the boat. He still hung his head. Meg came over and sat on Luke's knee. She told her that Harley wanted to be alone. He was worried it was over between them. Just then Luke saw that the girl was trying her luck again.

"Why is she still persisting in this? He's said no. Just let it go already." Luke sounded so angry about it. "I best go save him."

"No, I'll go," Lizzie said adamantly. She got up, straightened her clothes and hair, almost preparing herself for a fight and confidently strolled over. Lizzie stepped between Harley and the girl, making sure to face the girl. Lizzie was going to stand up for her man, fight for her man and stand up to her. The girl was slightly taller than Lizzie, but at this point, Lizzie just didn't care.

The girl became very frustrated that Lizzie had intervened and got right up close to her. "Back off. He's mine!" she ordered.

Lizzie laughed. "All this effort and this is the best you can come up with!" Lizzie stood firm. All she could think of was how she wasn't about to lose Harley, the love of her life, especially to someone like her. No matter how long it had been, Lizzie knew her love for Harley was strong, and she was going to fight to keep it.

Lizzie didn't budge. The girl came closer. She was even trying to flirt with him around Lizzie. Every attempt that was made, Lizzie blocked. Harley placed his hand on Lizzie's shoulder and it seemed to give her a burst of confidence. In a calm and clear voice, Lizzie made a little speech. "I'm his girlfriend and nothing you do is going to change that. Whatever you try will *not* succeed. You have been told several times by him and his mate to leave them alone, so it is about time you paid attention. Leave the four of us alone." Lizzie said the last part one word at a time, each with emphasis and she took a step forward. They were almost touching at this point and Lizzie's expression was stern.

As soon as Lizzie finished her little speech, Harley leant down and whispered, "You're amazing." He spun her round, pulled her in tightly, and locked his lips on hers. He wasn't going to let go anytime soon. The kiss was only broken when the boat's horn sounded, making Lizzie jump. The girl had walked off by this point.

They collected their things and disembarked. Harley didn't let go of Lizzie's hand the whole time. When they walked to their seats in the coach, the girls gave Lizzie such a glare. Sitting down, Harley finally said something. "I'm sorry about this and thank you."

"I love you and your love for me makes me feel stronger. I knew I had to help you and thought I also needed to prove to you that this incident wouldn't affect us."

"I'm glad you did. I was very worried it was going to cause things to end between us."

"Harley, some girl trying it on with you is not going to change my mind about you. I know it's not been long enough really, but I trust you. And although it was a big shock to see it, I still trust you."

Harley sighed. "I never want to lose you, Lizzie."

"I never want to lose you either. You're mine and always will be."

Harley sat against the window this time. He pulled Lizzie right into him, leaning back against the window. He spent the rest of the coach ride cuddling her tightly and he kept kissing her forehead. Lizzie felt so happy wrapped up in his arms, and each time he kissed her, she shivered from the surge of electricity pulsing through her.

In reception back at the complex, the girls confronted Harley and Lizzie. Meg and Luke came up to stand with them. Harley had been holding Lizzie's hand and his grip became stronger. Lizzie took a small step forward. "Why do you keep thinking you have a shot with my boyfriend?"

"Your boyfriend? Maybe in your dreams!" She was laughing, and her friend was agreeing and laughing too.

"Really, why would you think that? You've seen how we are together." Lizzie stepped forward. "You saw us in the coach cuddling up and you think we are not an item?"

"Whatever! He'll be mine by tomorrow."

"You need to leave him, and us four, alone."

Eventually the two girls left, and Lizzie let out a massive sigh of relief. Harley pulled her into him. "You were great."

"Until they start up the next time we bump into them."

Harley and Luke didn't leave their sides for the rest of

the day. They all enjoyed dinner together and that night they split into couples again. Harley and Luke hadn't wanted to leave the girls, and Lizzie and Meg hadn't want to leave the guys either.

They went via the bar to collect a drink each to take back to the rooms. The girls from the boat had been in the bar, so while waiting for the drinks to be poured, Harley made an exaggerated effort, putting his arm around Lizzie and giving her a long, wild, open-mouthed kiss.

Chapter 15

Karaoke Night

For the next few days, they all hung out together, never leaving each other alone for more than a few minutes. They played pool, volleyball and tennis. They swam together and the couples enjoyed lots of cuddles in and around the pool. Harley and Lizzie even took Luke and Meg to the air rifle place, enjoying a friendly competition. They had bumped into the girls a lot. They must have arrived the weekend before the boat trip as they hadn't seen them previously. Thankfully, so far, they had not tried anything with Harley or Luke since. However, it had been funny seeing them trying their luck with other guys. What made it even funnier was that they failed with every attempt.

Eating dinner Wednesday evening, they talked about the fact that tomorrow was their last full day on holiday. The guys asked if they could take them on another date night. Lizzie and Meg agreed without hesitation. They got so overly excited at the prospect it caused Harley and Luke to laugh. They spent some nights during the last week of the holiday as couples and spent some nights in their own rooms. Tonight, with the anticipation of date night, they were going to be splitting off again.

Since the excursion, Lizzie and Meg had been walking the guys to their room before heading to their own. Harley and Luke didn't like it, but they let the girls have their way, on one condition: They had to call when they were back in their room. It made the girls laugh, but they agreed.

After dinner though, they first headed to the bar. It was karaoke night, and the girls had signed Harley and Luke up for a couple of songs each. They had heard so much about the band they played and sang in and now they wanted to hear those voices for themselves. They sat at a table close to the stage, which was all set up for the night about to start. Several songs into the evening, the DJ announced it was Harley's turn with "Don't Threaten Me with a Good Time" by Panic! At the Disco. Harley shot a questioning look at Luke, who just shrugged. "It wasn't me."

"Sorry. It was me," Lizzie said with a massive smile. "I really want to hear you sing."

Harley gave her a quick peck on the lips and headed to the stage.

He stood tall on the stage; he seemed full of confidence. He took the mic from the stand and held it close to his lips as the song started. He hardly looked at the words screen, yet he was word perfect and sounded amazing. People who had not really been paying any attention so far had come closer to the stage. Many of them were girls who noticed this attractive guy on stage. Harley, however, was not paying attention to anyone but Lizzie. It was as if he was singing to her and only her. When the song ended, everyone stood to applause, including Lizzie, Luke and Meg. Harley smiled at them. At that point he realised how big a crowd he had drawn. He smiled, waved and took a bow.

"Wow, excellent karaoke. And if you're following that performance, then I am sorry," said DJ before announcing the next singer. "Next we have Luke with 'Friday, I'm in Love' by The Cure."

Luke looked at Meg and winked, "Anything for you." He knew it was Meg's favourite song and was happy that she had chosen it for him to sing to her. He gave her a kiss before heading up. His energy and confident shone with each stride. Harley and Luke crossed paths and Luke slapped Harley on the shoulder in a brotherly hug. Harley's face cringed as Luke caught the claw mark Lizzie had given him. "Oh, sorry mate."

"It's OK. I hope you sing this better than you sing in the band," Harley joked. Harley took his seat next to Lizzie as the song began. Luke was even more confident than Harley with singing, but then he was the lead singer for the band.

Just as the song was starting Luke announced, "This is dedicated to my amazing and sexy girlfriend, Meg." As he said it, he raised his arm in Meg's direction. Then he started to sing.

Lizzie looked over at Meg. She had tears rolling down her cheeks. Lizzie nudged Harley, nodding towards Meg. He smiled. "Likes the song that much, does she?" he joked.

Luke's voice was as amazing as Harley's, but Luke had more showmanship than Harley. Both girls were ecstatic.

When Luke returned, the girls told them they had another song lined up for them both. They didn't mind one bit. Then they went to the bar to fetch more drinks. There were a few girls who commented on their singing and flirted with them. The girls from the boat tried their luck again, but all the guys did was smile, say thank you to the compliments and returned with the drinks to their girlfriends.

For the next hour, they laughed, drank and danced to the other karaoke songs. Some were good, some were cringe worthy and a few were horrifyingly bad. Then Harley's next song was announced. He walked up; the DJ greeted him again with a thankful smile. The song Lizzie had chosen for Harley this time was "Last Resort" by Papa Roach. She knew from their discussions over the last two weeks that they were one of his favourite bands and he played this song quite a lot. Again he held the mic, and throughout the whole song, his foot and one of his hands looked like they were trying to play the drums as they beat along to the rhythm.

Harley stopped and chatted with the DJ for a few minutes before returning to the table. Next it was Luke's turn with, "Are You Gonna Be My Girl" by Jet. Meg was on her feet ready to dance before the song even started. Luke was amazing and he got everyone riled up. Everyone was dancing and clapping along.

Straight after Luke's song finished, the DJ announced, "I have been asked by the best two singers of this karaoke to allow an extra song. As they are the best, I have accepted. Please welcome to the stage Harley and Luke, along with their girlfriends, Lizzie and Meg, to sing 'Summer of 69' by Brian Adams."

Everyone was on their feet clapping. Luke had stayed on stage and Harley bundled Lizzie and Meg up onto the stage. The girls felt rather embarrassed at first, but they had also had enough to drink to give them a confidence boost. The song started and Luke instantly got the crowd dancing and clapping again. The girls started to relax and sing along with the guys. They all happily sang away.

When the song finished, they took a bow. Everyone was clapping. They returned to their table with one more round of drinks as they listened to a few more songs before heading back to their rooms. When the girls got back to their room, they were still filled with excitement and energy. They put some music on and packed while singing and dancing round. After an hour though they were ready to collapse from exhaustion. They quietened down, turned the music off and got ready for bed.

"Luke was amazing. He got everyone going," Lizzie said.

"I know. I was so impressed. I hadn't expected it. Harley was amazing too."

Lizzie smiled. "Yes, his voice was wonderful. I think I'm going to have to make him sing to me again tomorrow night."

"Ooh, I hadn't thought of that. I might suggest that too."

Chapter 16

The Final Day

Lizzie and Meg spent the next day together. They played tennis, hung about at the pool, went for plenty of swims to cool down, sampled more of the mocktails and did plenty of reading. It was a lovely, relaxing day and the trouble with the girls seemed to have been forgotten. After lunch they played pool for a little while, where Luke and Harley found them. The problem girls were in the bar also. Harley walked right up to Lizzie. He wrapped his arms around her, embracing her tightly, and gave her a loving kiss. The exaggerated embrace was an act for the girls but the way he held her and the kiss were because he had missed her.

"Tables are booked for seven o'clock, and then I'm taking you back to my bed," Harley declared. He leant in, kissed her neck and whispered in her ear, "I'm really looking forward to making love to you tonight and cuddling with you all night long."

Lizzie smiled and squeezed him back. She was also looking forward to that.

They enjoyed a few rounds of pool together and continued to sample the mocktails list. The girls had tried each one several times over the last week. Throughout the holiday, Harley had been teaching Lizzie how to play pool, always taking the opportunity to improve her stance, hold of the cue or angle of her shot. All had to be done by him standing right next to her or physically adjusting her position. The lesson Lizzie liked the best was when he leant over her to help her angle her shot better. She used to ask for his help, even if she didn't need it, just so he would lean over her and press his body against her.

Harley and Luke went off to play tennis, while Lizzie and Meg went back to their books. By time they went back to their room, they had just finished their third book of the holiday. "I can't believe we have only just finished our third book," Meg started.

"I know. The guys have been so distracting!" Lizzie joked. They had a laugh and continued to chat, talking about the books they had finished. They liked hearing about the books the other had read and most of the time they ended up swapping books.

Lizzie and Meg were getting ready in their room when the usual knock sounded at the door. Meg was still walking round in her underwear and Lizzie was still drying and styling her hair. They checked the time, thinking that they were running late. "They're earlier than normal," Meg commented.

Wrapped in her towel, Lizzie went to open the door. Harley stood there with a bottle of sparkling in his hands. Luke stood there with four glasses. They both looked handsome and smart.

"Gosh, you two look gorgeous. Come in. Make yourselves comfy." As she walked back into the bedroom to finish getting ready, Lizzie heard the pop of the cork. Meg had her dress on now and was almost ready, so she went through to get glasses for them both.

When it was time to leave for the restaurant, they had gone through the whole bottle. Throughout the meal Lizzie kept rubbing her foot up and down Harley's leg, and she kept finding herself biting her lip. They were talking a lot and held hands between every course. When dessert arrived, Lizzie took a forkful and raised it to Harley's lips. As he leant forward to take it, she moved closer and whispered flirtatiously, "I'm not sure how much longer I can control myself. Your smell is intoxicating; your touch is electrifying. And you need to stop looking at me that way, or I won't be held responsible for what happens next."

As she said that last part, she ran her foot up his leg and along his thigh. He swallowed hard and took a deep breath. She could see him start to shake. He took her hand, leant in and kissed her. Breathlessly he said, "I want you now! We need to go."

She just smiled. It was the response she wanted, but she was going to tease him. So she slowly finished her dessert. She caressed the chocolate with her tongue or pulled the fork out of her mouth slowly before biting her lip. "If you continue with this, we are going to leave before you've finished that," threatened Harley.

"OK," she said, and abruptly stood up. Lizzie had almost finished, but as they hadn't spent last night cuddled up together, she wanted him as badly as he wanted her.

They left the restaurant in a hurry and ran, laughing, back to his room. They noticed the problem girls walking out of their room. They saw Harley and just stopped and stared. Harley smiled at Lizzie, picked her up and as her legs wrapped around him, he slammed her to his room door. He pressed his body firmly against her, making her gasp. They were in a lip lock battle, fervently kissing. He was concentrating on Lizzie so much that he struggled to put the key in the lock. She turned her head, looking at the lock long enough for him to put the key in and unlock the door. Then using his now-free hand, he turned her head back to kiss her some more. As the door opened, Lizzie was no longer pinned. She backed off from him a little so she could focus on his eyes. She smiled at him and just happened to catch a glimpse of the girls, still standing there, still staring. Lizzie straightened a little more and focused properly. Harley stopped, looked at her, and followed her gaze. The girl who had tried to make out with Harley looked annoyed. Harley didn't care. He went back to kissing Lizzie's neck and running his fingers through her hair. He pushed the door open fully, walked into his room, and kicked the door shut. Then he carried her straight to his bed.

He had been kissing her neck and trying to find the zip on her dress. He had struggled to find the zip all the way from the door to his bed. "It's on the side," she finally told him, lifting one of her arms. He lowered her down and undid the zip, placing the dress gently on Luke's bed. He stripped her before wrapping his arms around her and laying her on the bed. He placed some of his weight on her body and her want of him intensified. He got off her for a moment, striped completely and put on the protection before he climbed slowly back on top of her. He lavished kisses on every part of her. He placed his body weight on her again, just enough to make her gasp out of desire.

Her legs were wrapped around him, pulling him in as firmly as possible. There was no rush tonight, but they couldn't help it. They were both filled with the desire for each other that had to be satisfied. They didn't want anything but the deep, passionate connection that making love would satisfy. As he brushed his body along her body, he entered and their bodies pulsated together. Their hunger and their desire for each other meant that every movement which brought their bodies clashing together needed to become firmer. Each motion became firmer, harder and deeper, but it still didn't seem enough. Her nails scratched down his back several times and at one point made him moan out suddenly. It was a mix of pain and pleasure. Her nails had caused scratch marks to appear, but that just turned things up a notch. By the end, the bed was repeatedly colliding with the wall. They were moaning and groaning so loudly it could probably be heard ten rooms away.

Harley was reaching his climax, his thrusts became harder and deeper but slower. At the same time, he locked his lips on Lizzie's and they waved through their shared climaxes, swallowing their moans before they both collapsed, exhausted from their wild and untamed session.

Harley moved off Lizzie and rolled on to his back, letting out a sudden, "Ah." A painful expression scrunched up his face.

"You OK?" Lizzie asked.

"It's just my shoulder. It just hurt when I leant down," he said casually, thinking nothing of it.

"Let me take a look."

Harley turned onto his front to let Lizzie have a look as to what could have just caused his discomfort. Lizzie's cringed when she saw what damage her nails had done again. Harley had three new scratches running from his neck and across his shoulder blade. "Oh my, Harley. I'm sorry. I got you really good when I scratched you. You've got another three scratches."

"You little minx. Do I need to get my own back on you now?"

Lizzie could see him smiling, despite his face being partially buried into the pillow. She kissed along all five scratches from the top to the bottom. Harley let out a contented, breathy sigh. Lizzie continued to kiss all over his back. She could tell he was enjoying the sensations. His muscles were twitching. His sighs and moans were increasing in frequency and intensity, at which point he tried to move so he could kiss her. Lizzie moved her body to put her weight on his hips and held his shoulders down with her hands. He was pressed into the pillow and with no easy way of moving, so he gave in and just enjoyed the sensations she was creating.

She relaxed her pressure on his shoulders and ran her fingers down his spine. His back arched as a deep, long moan escaped his lips. She dragged her tongue up his spine and as she reached his neck, she proceeded to kiss and nibble along his unscratched shoulder and up his neck, stopping to nibble on his earlobe. Harley was enjoying every pleasurable sensation caused by every touch and didn't make any effort to move for a long while. The pleasure he felt led to arousal, and he repeatedly tried to kiss her. After a while, Lizzie let him.

He pulled her down next to him so he could reciprocate the sensations he had just experienced. His fingers slowly and tenderly ran through her hair and then down her cheek all the way to her waist, where he pulled her in tight. He placed one of his thighs between hers before tilting them round so he was back on top. Within moments he had put on protection. But he continued with his teasing, gentle strokes leaving fiery trails across her body. The whole time their lips locked together, demonstrating their passion for each other. Lizzie was stroking his good side with her fingers, but on his scratched side, she held his waist tight, trying not to move her hand. It all got the better of her eventually, though and her fingers trailing round his back. As her fingers caught the scratches, he let out a gasp as his clenching muscles caused his shoulders to arch back, and his hips were thrust firmly against her. It was a mixture of pleasure and pain each time she caught them.

At one point her knees were raised, her legs wrapped round him as their bodies rocked together and she accidently caught the scratches again. This time the sudden sensation rushing through his body caused his hips to thrust forward, crashing against her. During this movement he entered her and they both let out a long and most satisfying moan. Their bodies pulsed together with the waves of passion that were coursing through them. She grabbed him firmly as a second intense wave took hold of her. This time, though, her arms were wrapped round his shoulders and his body surged with the painful pleasure again. Things built from there, everything becoming firmer, deeper and harder until they again climaxed together.

They rested for a moment to regain control of their bodies before freshening up and getting drinks. Harley was trying to see the scratches in the mirror; he could just about see either end. Lizzie fetched the mirror from the lounge and held it for him to see them properly.

"I'm sorry" she said.

He turned round, placed the mirror aside, and embraced her. "It's OK. It's only a couple of scratches. Let's just hope it's not as painful tomorrow."

Lizzie looked at the ground. She looked and felt very guilty. It was the second time she caused damage because she was too engrossed with the sensations and his touch. Harley tilted her chin up so he could look directly into her eyes. "It's fine, I'm fine. They are only scratches, and Lizzie, despite how they look, I loved every minute. Plus now I can tell all my mates I have a gorgeous, sexy tiger of a girlfriend, and they will *all* be jealous," he joked.

They returned to bed and cuddled closely, legs tangled and his arms wrapped around her. She had one arm draped over him. The other was buried, pressed against his chest. She could feel his heart beating and gave him a kiss. "If this is what we are like after two nights of not being cuddled in the same bed, what are we going to be like after a week, let alone a month or whole semester?" she asked.

"I know. I'm not sure how I'm going to go a whole day without being able give you a kiss or hug," Harley commiserated.

"FaceTime is going to have to do, but it's going to be difficult, very difficult."

"I can't believe tomorrow night we will be on a flight home. I can't even begin to imagine how I'm going to feel when we land and have to go our separate ways," he said sadly and quietly.

"Don't get me started on that. I get so sad if I think about it."

"Well then, what time shall I come round to yours on the Saturday? Will nine o'clock be early enough?"

During their many conversations they had discovered they only lived about thirty minutes from each other. His parents' house was in the countryside. They owned a farm and his mum owned and ran the spa next door.

"Not soon enough," Lizzie joked. Then she continued in a more serious tone. "Isn't that a little early, though? We are on a late-night flight, so it will be really late by time we both get to our homes. Plus I need you to be well rested so you have plenty of stamina. Can't have you running out of energy by time we get into bed."

"Hey, I've not run out of stamina so far. I'll be up at seven easy. Luke and I usually go for a run at that time, so I'm happy to get to yours just after eight."

"I'll take eight in that case then." Lizzie was so happy that she couldn't stop smiling. Harley was smiling just as excitedly.

"I'll pack us a lunch and when you arrive, we can go for that hike and picnic," she said.

"Sounds perfect."

Chapter 17

The Sorrowful Flight Home

Harley had set an alarm for the morning as they needed to pack and get out of the rooms before lunch. The four enjoyed breakfast together before they went their separate ways for a bit. Lizzie and Meg had done some packing the day before, just leaving out the essentials and things they used yesterday. They packed the rest of their things and opened the door to take the cases to reception. Harley and Luke were standing outside their room, arms raised as they were about to knock. They took the cases and walked to reception; their things were already in storage. Lizzie was surprised they got everything packed so quickly, thinking that they probably just dumped everything in their cases and zipped them up, hoping for the best.

With cases locked away in the reception storage, they went to lunch. There were five hours before the coach was leaving for the airport. They enjoyed a nice long lunch, went for a walk along the beach and hung around the bar. The coach arrived late in the afternoon and they watched to make sure their cases went into the coach. They saw Lizzie's and Meg's, and a little while later, another case got loaded. "That's ours," said Harley.

"So that's why it didn't take you long to pack. You didn't have much to pack," remarked Lizzie.

"Well we were coming from one address, so what's the point in having loads. And we are men. Plus we didn't expect to meet anyone on holiday, so we didn't really bring loads with us."

"Men? Are you sure? You don't act like it," Lizzie said with a huge smile on her face. Lizzie and Meg fell about laughing while Harley and Luke looked severely unimpressed.

"Charming. Maybe I should tell them about my brutal girlfriend then," Harley joked.

"I'm surprised you haven't told Luke already!"

"What have we missed?" Luke and Meg both asked together.

"Things got a bit hot and heavy last night and she scratched the hell out of my back. Again!"

"I did not," Lizzie said defensively and then got a little quieter. "Well I did scratch him. He's got three lovely new scratches on his shoulder."

Harley whipped off his T-shirt to show Luke. Meg saw and just looked at Lizzie. "Wow!"

"Bet that was painful, Hars."

"It was after, when I went to lay down," Harley said putting his top back on.

Arriving at the airport they went straight to the bar in the departures. They were starving. They ordered some food and drinks and sat chatting, laughing, and cuddling. They tried not to think about going their separate ways after they landed. Lizzie did end up thinking about it, sometimes, and she became a little saddened by it. Harley realised it every time. He pulled her in for a little squeeze and gave a kiss every time. That certainly took her mind off things.

Meg boarded first and found the seats on their tickets, Harley asked Lizzie if she would sit next to him and let Luke have her seat. "As if you have to ask."

"Great! Luke asked me earlier. He was a little shy about asking you to swap."

"Plenty of cuddles for us then. To be honest, Meg and I had discussed trading seats, so we could sit with you both."

Harley and Lizzie continued along the aisle to the seats he and Luke were meant to have, leaving Luke snuggling up with Meg.

Harley and Lizzie cuddled up and listened to some rock music together. He had been trying to introduce her to heavy metal. She had liked some of the bands, but some songs she couldn't understand what they were screaming about. Harley told her they weren't really his style either; he had just wanted to see her reaction. Lizzie fell asleep on his shoulder for a while and he cuddled her in close, trying to make sure she was comfortable. Waking up she asked Harley how long she had been asleep. "Only about twenty minutes."

"Oh, that's OK. I was worried I'd missed most the flight time with you."

They spent the rest of the journey cuddling, kissing and just being together. Neither of them could believe how this holiday romance had turned into a love that meant everything to them both.

After landing, they all got a little sad. They collected their cases in silence, sad expressions on their faces. Harley managed to cheer Lizzie up though. "I'll be at yours in about twelve hours."

Lizzie smiled and took Harley's hand which he had offered her. Luke and Meg couldn't meet up quite as soon.

Meg had family commitments tomorrow, but she was seeing him on the Sunday. Harley and Luke took all three cases off the belt and placed them together on a trolley. They started to wheel the trolley through to arrivals, where Lizzie and Meg knew their parents would be waiting.

"We can take it from here if you'd like," Meg said very nervously.

"Nope, we are going to be gentlemen, help you with your cases, and make sure you get to your parents OK."

Lizzie and Meg looked at each other and smiled sort of timid, embarrassed smiles. They had told their parents they met Harley and Luke, but they hadn't mentioned anything too specific.

"Could I get my proper kiss now, before we go through?" Lizzie asked.

"Of course. Why?"

"I feel a little awkward kissing you in front of my parents."

"Are my kiss a little too passionate for you in that situation?"

She bit her lip. "You know me too well. I just haven't prepared my parents for you and us. They know I've met a nice guy on holiday, but that's all I've really told them."

He didn't reply. He just embraced her tightly and they locked their lips firmly together with a long and passionate kiss. He made it so passionate her knees went a little weak. Harley, feeling her knees weaken, increased his grip on her. As they came up for air, Harley laughed. "Take it that was passionate enough for you?"

Lizzie, still breathing heavily, could only manage a

smile. Then they noticed Luke and Meg in a lip lock too. They probably felt the same way.

Lizzie and Meg stood there, frozen by their nerves. The guys nudged them on, and as the girls took a step forward, they each took a deep breath. Harley walked next to Lizzie, pushing the trolley. He subtly offered his hand, which she took. Her grip tightened as she saw her and Meg's parents, who looked very excited to see their daughters back from holiday. But when Lizzie's parents saw that Harley and Lizzie were holding hands, their expressions became more questioning, more worried about what had actually gone on.

It was the mums who grabbed each girl first, giving a big hug and asking about their holiday. It was almost as if they were trying to ignore the fact that Harley and Luke were there. The girls had explained their parents to Harley and Luke as they had known something like this would probably happen. Harley took his case off the trolley. Lizzie's dad took the trolley and thanked him. But as he was about to turn his back on Harley, Harley said "You're welcome, Mr Webb."

That made him stop. He was a little shocked that he had been spoken to so politely. But mainly he was shocked that Harley had called him Mr Webb. Harley's appearance had given him a completely different first impression.

Lizzie introduced Harley to her parents. "This is my dad, Michael." Harley reached out to shake his hand, which he reciprocated. "And this is my mum, Susan."

"Nice to meet you, Mr and Mrs Webb. You have a wonderful daughter. Lizzie is an amazing person."

As he went to carry on the conversation, something caught his attention. "Oh," he said as a look of disappointment appeared on his face. Lizzie looked over but couldn't figure out what he had seen. "Luke, we're being beckoned," Harley continued. Luke looked over and then back at Harley with a sort of 'typical' smile.

"What is it?" Meg asked.

"Mum and Dad must be busy. They sent a driver," Luke explained.

"Will I still see you in the morning?" Lizzie asked Harley.

"Absolutely, I'll be counting the hours." He gave her a kiss right on the lips. But he didn't linger or make it as passionate as their normal kisses. It was just a nice quick peck, suitable for in front of parents.

"See you bright and early. Let me know when you're home safe," Harley said. Then he looked at her parents and said, "It was lovely to meet you, and I might see you at some point tomorrow." Then he quietly whispered in Lizzie's ear, "Sweet dreams. I love you," and gave her a small kiss on her cheek.

During all this Luke was meeting Meg's parents. They seemed to get on all right, and as they all walked to the car, Lizzie and Meg linked arms to discuss the parents' meetings. Meg said Luke was lovely, but she couldn't tell what her parents thought. They looked very uninterested and plain-faced. She was expecting the third degree in the car with a hundred questions. And so was Lizzie.

"I don't know how I'm going to answer their questions," Lizzie said. "I don't want to tell them how serious we have become so quickly. They will just brush it off, saying that I'm just being immature. But I also don't want to make them believe that in a few weeks it'll be over."

"I know, I'm the same."

Walking out of the airport, they saw Harley and Luke

getting into a dark Bentley. Lizzie and Meg looked at each other. "Oh my God," they said to each other.

"Did Luke mention money to you?"

"No. Harley to you?"

"No," she said. "Well not really, but I suppose he did imply something. He told me his mum owns and runs a spa next door to their house and they have farmland."

"Luke told me that his dad is the head vet at a practice. We spoke about it for a while, but that was more about the animal side of things. I wonder if they own that too."

"I'm going to find out tomorrow. I'll let you know straightaway."

The car journey home was painfully long. Her parents quizzed her about Harley the whole time. They already didn't like him and no matter what she said about him and how many questions she answered, they didn't seem to budge from that impression. By time they had got into the house, Lizzie felt like crying. They had just told her they were unhappy with her seeing him tomorrow. In fact, they were unhappy with her ever seeing him again.

"You haven't even given him a chance. You have no idea what he is like," Lizzie shouted, tears forming in her eyes.

"Nor do you. You were only on holiday for two weeks," Susan replied.

"Yes, I've only known him two weeks, which means that I know a lot more about him than you do in the two minutes you spoke to him. It's not fair to make a decision on someone when all he has done is to be polite."

Just then Lizzie's phone rang. It was Harley. "I'm going to bed, and I am going out with Harley tomorrow. And I won't be back until Sunday," she said as she stormed upstairs.

Lizzie and Harley spoke on the phone for a while. She was very happy to hear his kind, friendly voice, especially after the argument with her parents. She sat in silence for much of the conversation, and he was just talking to her, trying to make her smile, or at least feel better. But she continued to cry.

Lizzie was adamant that no matter what her parents thought, she was going to continue her relationship with Harley. With everything that had happened on holiday, there was no way that she was going to just stop seeing him.

Harley was still on the phone with her, and he told her to get ready for bed. He would ring her back in five minutes. She did as he said, and as she climbed into bed, he rang.

"You lying comfy?" he asked.

"Yes," she sobbed.

"Good. Close your eyes, and imagine that I'm there with you, my hand trailing up your spine."

She shivered from the sensations created by just imagining his touch.

"My fingers running through your hair and down your neck. I'm going to keep trailing my fingers up and down your back until you're asleep."

"I can't wait to see you in the morning."

"I'm counting down the hours, and I'm going to wrap my arms tightly round you and try to take all this pain away."

"You're so sweet to me, Harley. I love you."

"And I love you. Goodnight, hun."

"Goodnight, gorgeous," she said as she drifted to sleep.